Praise for Mackenzie McKade's *Lost But Not Forgotten*

5 Lips and a Recommended Read "In Lost but Not Forgotten, Mackenzie McKade delivers a strong and sexy heroine paired with a melt-in-your-mouth hero, and the combination is exquisite. ...The story's details add to the realism and will suck you in right from the first page. This book is phenomenal – a must read."

~ Lindy, Two Lips Review

5 Klovers "Mackenzie McKade has a reputation for the ability to make readers feel everything her characters feel. Her newest release, Lost But Not Forgotten, is a prime example of this talent! McKade ran us through the gamut of emotions in this book: fear, love, desire, pain, and more. ...Truly, it is the kind of writing that makes you forget these are fictional characters instead of friends, even if just for a short time."

~ Jennifer, Ck2S Kwips and Kritiques

5 Blue Ribbons "Mackenzie McKade delivers a touching story of love lost and found-literally. ...Alison's frustration, denial and anger are palpable in Ms. McKade's words."

~ Lynn, Fallen Angels

5 Blue Ribbons "Mackenzie McKade's LOST BUT NOT FORGOTTEN takes readers on an emotional journey along with the characters. ...LOST BUT NOT FORGOTTEN contains a combination of memorable characters, hot BDSM scenes and enough suspense to keep you engrossed in the story until the very end."

~ Crissy Dione, Romance Junkies

Lost But Not Forgotten

Mackenzie McKade

A Samhain Publishing, Ltd. publication.

Samhain Publishing, Ltd.
577 Mulberry Street, Suite 1520
Macon, GA 31201
www.samhainpublishing.com

Lost But Not Forgotten

Print ISBN: 978-1-59998-790-3
Digital ISBN: 1-59998-193-9

Editing by Angela James
Cover by Scott Carpenter

First Samhain Publishing, Ltd. electronic publication: July 2007
First Samhain Publishing, Ltd. print publication: May 2008

Dedication

It is with great pleasure that I dedicate this book to three people who have touched my life. Fate has made us siblings, but time has made us friends. Denese, Dub, and Tammie, thank you for believing in me.

Chapter One

The last thing Jake O'Malley ever thought he'd see was Alison Grant handcuffed to his bed.

He had imagined it—even dreamed of it. Yet in each of those dreams her expression had been soft with desire, so damn sexy he had woken from his fantasy spent and weak-kneed. Nothing like the fire-and-brimstone look on her face that made even Johnny Cane, one of Arizona's finest, and their childhood friend, take a step backward.

If looks could kill, Johnny was a dead man.

Of course, there was one detail Jake couldn't overlook—Allie was supposed to be dead or on the run.

Jake nearly dropped the box he held as his gaze slid over the agitated woman lying across his bed. More than enough leg was showing to make a man's pulse shift into overdrive. With just a brush of Jake's hand, he could push that little skirt higher to reveal the treasure he had dreamed of for years. His cock hardened with the thought of spreading her thighs and thrusting between them.

Damn. He had missed her.

Not to mention he was relieved more than words could say—she was alive. He'd been so worried about her this past year when he discovered that she'd disappeared off the face of the earth.

What trouble had the little minx got herself in?

After fire destroyed the compound in the Amazon and Allie couldn't be found, he and Mabel, Allie's mother, had spent twelve frantic months wondering if she was even alive. No telephone calls. No letters. Now, from out of nowhere, she showed up sprawled across his bed, looking better than ever before, making all his old feelings spring alive.

His mother had called it puppy love.

Jake knew differently.

Before he could reveal his feelings to Allie, she'd left without a good-bye on a mid-January afternoon, just like today. Packed her things and hightailed it out of Gilbert as fast as she could.

Hot resentment crawled up his neck, rushing straight to his ears, and then died quickly.

At least she was alive.

The sound of Johnny panting brought Jake's attention back to the frustrated man. Johnny's hat was cocked sidewise, revealing thick, red hair to match the flush on his cheeks. His usually crisp uniform was in disarray, shirt wrinkled and dislodged from his pants. He sported some angry red marks around his throat. Johnny returned Allie's hot glare as he stuffed his shirt back into his pants.

"Allie—" he breathed angrily, "—dammit. I told you to settle down."

"Fuck you," she spat with enough heat to singe the ends of Johnny's hair. The image almost made Jake laugh. "What the hell's going on here? What are those men doing with my mother's curio cabinet?"

That was Allie. React first and ask questions later. However, in this case it looked like Johnny had won.

Still, Jake couldn't get over seeing her again. Relief swished through his lungs.

She's alive. His palms itched to touch her, make sure she wasn't just a vision like the ones that visited him every night.

Dammit. Where have you been, Allie? He wanted to scream the question, but he wasn't yet ready to reveal his presence. Quietly, he eased back into the hallway, keeping her within his sight.

Caught between wanting to hold or strangle her, he eyed the beauty again, thinking how nice it would be to have her really handcuffed to his bed—the new one to be delivered this weekend. She adjusted herself, sitting sideways on her hip, which resulted in baring more leg. Life stirred again between his thighs, tightening his jeans across his hips. It didn't take much for him to imagine her naked, each limb stretched tight and bound to the bedposts. Would she moan or whimper softly as he traced a flogger down her delicate skin? In his mind's eye, he could hear the crack of the whip and her sweet cry when he marked her.

Visions of her spread wide for his pleasure nearly stole his breath. He had waited a lifetime to have her where she now lay, but it wasn't going to happen, at least not at the moment.

Get a grip on yourself. But Jake's thoughts were running amok. His furry red handcuffs would look better than the cold gray ones that now adorned Allie's wrists. The matching ankle bracelets would be a nice addition.

Narrow-eyed, she tossed her head, sending a mass of long, wheaten curls behind her. "*Johnny.*" There was something scary in her tone as it dropped in pitch to almost a growl. "If you want to see another sunrise, you'll remove these cuffs." Her nostrils flared, but it was her chest that Jake couldn't keep his eyes off.

Holy shit. He had forgotten just how well-endowed Allie was. The first four buttons were missing from her white silk blouse, displaying deep cleavage he had dreamed of trailing his tongue down more than once. The swells of her full globes trimmed in white lace made him ache to see more. He shifted the box from one arm to the other and wondered if her panties matched her bra. The short leather skirt she wore was raised just enough to tease a man, but revealed nothing more than her long, slender legs. Leather boots up to her knees made him redirect his focus to her thighs.

Damn. Jake couldn't think when he was around Allie. Even after all these years. The only thought he could muster was parting Allie's thighs and tasting what had never been his. The arousing scent of her flowery perfume, lilies, wasn't helping things.

Johnny rubbed his throat with agitation. "Now, Allie. Just listen to me. Your mama...well...this isn't your house anymore."

She jerked against her restraints, and the brass bed cried out in dismay beneath her. "Bullshit," she spat, releasing all her fury behind it. "Has everyone lost their friggin' minds?"

Her fingers splayed, then curled into ten sharp claws that Jake, as well as Johnny, knew she would use if given the chance. Probably the reason she wore handcuffs. Johnny knew her too well.

"Aaargh..." She pushed a heavy breath from her parted lips before pinning her steely gaze on Johnny. He shifted his weight from foot to foot, trying to look away.

When she grew quiet, Johnny took a step backward.

By the deep-set lines etching her forehead, Jake could imagine the wheels spinning in her head. She was thinking, and that wasn't a good sign for any of them, especially Jake once she discovered he had purchased her ancestral home and all its contents.

Fact was, he couldn't see the house he had come to feel as his home away from home sold to a stranger. Since he was being honest, at least to himself, he admitted it made him feel a little closer to the young girl who had left four years ago on an adventure and had taken his heart with her.

Yeah. Sure. Allie hadn't even known he existed as more than a friend. But he definitely knew she did. He wasn't that shy, four-eyed bookworm anymore.

"*Johnny.*" This time the officer's name was a purr upon her full lips. Thick eyelashes swept her high cheekbones before her big blue eyes softened. "Johnny. Please let me go. We can resolve this issue calmly." Her thighs inched slightly apart, immediately drawing Johnny's attention.

Wicked wench. Jake shook his head, a smile teasing the corners of his mouth.

Allie was all woman.

In the right frame of mind, she wasn't afraid to use it to her advantage.

Johnny swallowed hard. "Ahhh...Allie." He took a step toward her.

Sucker, Jake chuckled inwardly. Johnny always fell for her tricks. Hell, she had perfected them on the poor boy when they were kids.

It was always the same thing with this woman. She was like a bull in a china store, first trying to muscle her way through a situation. When brawn didn't work, she turned on her sensuality and it was end of story. You'd think by now she'd learn to try that approach first. Every man fell under her spell.

Jake was no exception—until now.

Shifting the box in his arms, he squared his shoulders. This time if she wanted something from him, it would cost her. Alison Grant was not leaving town until he had sampled what he had yearned for since they were in high school. But more importantly, he needed to know where she'd been this last year. He'd spent many sleepless nights worrying about her.

As Johnny reached into his pocket for the handcuff keys, Jake said, "Isn't this cozy?"

Allie's eyes grew large as he strolled further into the room. His boots scuffed across the hardwood flooring.

"Jake?"

He couldn't tell if that was a Jake-I-can't-believe-it's-you or a Jake-what-the-hell-are-you-doing-here tone as his name left her mouth.

Johnny moved toward Jake. He leaned close and whispered, "I don't think she knows about her mama."

Anxiety slithered across Jake's skin. "Dammit, Johnny. You didn't tell her?" The last thing he wanted to do was to break the news to Allie her mother had died while she'd been missing.

"Nope. She didn't give me much of an opportunity. Came apart at the seams when she saw her mother's curio cabinet being hauled out the front door." Johnny rubbed the agitated marks around his neck. "You know Allie." He paused. "I think I'll let you tell her." A finger to the rim of his cap, he gave a little salute.

"Coward," Jake mumbled. Yet he didn't know if he would have handled it any different if he'd been here when she arrived. Moving sucked. He had a shit-load of packing to do.

"Oh, I didn't tell her who owns her mother's house either." Unease crept across the officer's face. "If you need me I'll be downstairs getting the rest of the boxes out of my car." He tossed the handcuff keys to Jake. Jake nearly dropped the box as he caught the keys with one hand. "Nice seeing you again, Allie. Uhhh...my condolences," Johnny said with a sad look before he exited through the open door.

Allie's frown deepened. "Condolences? What did he mean by that?"

Well, shit.

Jake took several steps, closing the distance between them. This was awkward. He didn't want to be the one to tell Allie about her mother. There was no telling how she'd react.

Delay.

"You look good in handcuffs, Allie." She'd be shocked to know the ideas that went through his head about her. He wanted to fuck her and leave his mark upon her body and soul. But then, he had always wanted that, ever since high school. Somewhat of a nerd, he did a lot of reading in those days—a lot. His taste in educational material spanned beyond the porn young boys enjoyed. He found early in life the desire to experiment with handcuffs and whips and toys of all sorts. It wasn't a lifestyle. He didn't get off being called Master or humiliating his partner. It was just that kink was a complete turn-on.

Always his fantasies included Allie.

She had such fire inside her, a glow he would have given anything to feel shine on him.

Allie slid her thighs together and cocked a brow. "What do you know about all this?"

Just like her to cut right to the point. No chit-chat. With Allie a straight line was always the shortest distance.

The muscles in his neck clenched. "It's good to see you too." Sarcasm edged his words, but he couldn't help it. She might not have thought about him all these years. Yet she had never been far from his mind or dreams. Every woman he made love to had her face.

The chains on the manacles jingled as she yanked against the restraints once more. She leveled her eyes on him. "What the hell is going on here? Where's Mom?"

The loose buttons that had popped off her shirt during her struggle with Johnny lay on the bed beside her legs. She still had a scar on her left knee where they had coasted together down the rocky water slide in Sedona at Slide Rock. The injury hadn't been bad, but it left a scar. They were twelve at the time and Mabel had invited Jake to visit Sedona with her and Allie. He had never met her father, seemed he skipped out on Mabel when she was pregnant with Allie.

Her life had been so very different from his. Yeah, he had a mother and father, but both were career-minded individuals, never having time for him. He had spent more time with Mabel and Allie than his own family.

They were a true family, doing everything together—even dreaming. Mabel had encouraged Allie to leave this town and experience the world, something she had never gotten the opportunity to do. The woman had lived through the spirited and exciting letters she received each week from Allie.

Jake mentally shook his wandering thoughts from his head and tightened his grip on the box he held in one arm. No one, not Mabel's lawyer or the private investigators Brayer Tech had hired, had been able to locate Allie. Even Mabel had hired someone to find Allie. It was as if she had literally vanished. There'd been no way for anyone to tell Allie that her mother had passed away.

"If you're through examining my legs, maybe you can tell me what's going on. Where's Mom?"

His gaze snapped to hers. “Mabel’s gone, Allie.” *Crap.* He hadn’t meant to blurt it out like that.

She was in the midst of tossing her hair over her shoulder when his words stopped her cold. Once again, her gaze narrowed. “Gone where?”

He took a step closer, unsure of what to say or do next. “This last year wasn’t a good one for her.” He pushed his fingers through his dark, short hair. The handcuff keys brushed against his forehead. “Worrying about you. Then her heart—” He wet his now dry lips, and then slipped the keys into his pocket.

Allie pulled her legs further beneath her and leaned forward against her restraints, her voice notching up. “What are you saying, Jake?”

Jake sucked in a tight breath. *Sonofabitch.* He didn’t want to do this. “She passed away two weeks ago.”

An expression of bewilderment slid across Allie’s face. Blindly she stared at him. Her silence was almost eerie. She didn’t blink—didn’t move. He’d even swear she wasn’t breathing.

“Allie?” Concern made him set the box on the floor and step closer. Before he reached the bed, the color in her face had drained to a ghastly pallor. In a chain reaction, first her head began to nod, small uncontrollable movements that filtered through her body, until they shook her entirely.

“No,” she gasped. The small sound, filled with agony, tightened his chest as he sat beside her.

Her misty eyes met his. Yet, there was something odd about the emptiness he saw reflecting back at him. These weren’t the same innocent eyes he had gazed into when they were young.

"Jake." She choked his name just before her chin began to quiver and a river of tears erupted. Her sorrow was heartbreaking.

Jake didn't know what to do. He reached out and touched her arm, and a panic-stricken look overtook her.

"I can't breathe," she wheezed. "I— "

As if a wrecking ball had smashed into her, he watched Allie crumble.

Her eyes flew wide and wild. Jerking and fighting her bindings, she fought to break free. Unladylike snorts and growls came from her pretty mouth, which shrieked "*Momma*." The gut-wrenching scream tore from deep within her chest, a release of the obvious anguish she experienced.

"Allie, please." Jake wrapped his arms around her and tried to keep her still. She was hurting herself. The cuffs were biting into her wrists, leaving red marks. "Baby, please."

She thrashed against him. Her cries were tearing him apart. There wasn't anything he could do, but hold her. It seemed like forever before she gave up her struggle, buried her face into his shoulder and wept.

"Everything okay?" Jake looked up to see Johnny standing in the doorway. Concern drew his friend's brows together. "You all right, Allie?"

She never acknowledged him, only pressed closer to Jake. He firmed his embrace, kissing her softly on the forehead.

"Jake, I left those boxes you asked for in the living room." Jake had helped Johnny move last month. Johnny was returning the favor by dropping his excess boxes off on his way to work. "If you don't need me, I'm taking off. Remember, after work today I'm on vacation. I'll be gone for about three weeks. The Caribbean is calling me." The laughter in Johnny's voice died. He stroked Allie with another anxious gaze. “Sorry about your mama.”

Jake gave his friend a nod. “Thanks, Johnny. Have fun in the Caribbean.”

Using one hand, Jake fished the keys out of his pocket. He released Allie long enough to unlocked the cuffs. Wrists free, she wrapped her arms around his neck and held on like she would never let go.

If only it were real.

Chapter Two

Mom is dead.

The knowledge was a dull knife through Allie's heart as she clung to Jake. The ache was something she wasn't prepared for—was anyone ever prepared to hear that their mother was gone?

Through the pain in her chest making it hard to breathe, she realized now Johnny had been trying to explain what had happened.

A fresh wave of emotions swamped her. Her body sagged against Jake.

Her mother was gone—a mother it took months to remember she had, before she mentally and physically recovered while lost in the rainforest of the Amazon. Hell, Allie hadn't even known her own name or that she had a life waiting for her.

A sob rippled through her.

Jake whispered, "I'm sorry, Allie." He held her so tightly, so safely.

How did everything get so messed up?

All Allie knew for sure was one day she was a documentarian for Brayer Tech, a large pharmaceutical company conducting medical research near the Pogo area in

Peru. The next day she woke to a sea of brown faces. English was definitely not the native tribe's language.

Jake brushed her hair from her face and attempted to give her a smile that fell short. "You okay?"

Allie turned her head, slowly taking in the familiar room—her mother's room. The same old blue curtains hung from the window. The dresser next to the bathroom door was littered with memorabilia, and pictures of trips they'd taken to Disneyland, Sedona, and Tombstone. Even the small brown pot that Allie had spun in a pottery class sat next to her mother's perfume bottle. Dust lingered on the wooden floor where the curio cabinet had stood. Her mother's favorite scent of roses lingered.

Another round of tears swelled in her eyes. "No. I'm not okay." Her pain streamed down her cheeks.

Her mother was gone.

Allie wouldn't be here today if it hadn't been for the Machiguengas. They nursed her back to health after finding her unconscious by the riverbank, miles away from her campsite and deep into the jungle.

She choked on a silent cry, not wanting to believe the truth she saw on Jake's face. The sadness that rimmed his eyes said he mourned too.

Every inch of her body felt heavy, pulling her deeper and deeper into the darkness surrounding and threatening to consume her.

"H—how, Jake?"

"Heart attack." His warm breath tickled her neck.

She closed her tear-spiked eyelashes. "I—I didn't know she was sick."

"Mabel and I tried to find you. The investigator Brayer hired turned up nothing. So we hired our own—still nothing. The last your mother knew you had disappeared along with some records."

Allie didn't know till recently that she was Brayer's number one suspect. The night of her disappearance, several employees' huts, including hers, were burned to the ground. Valuable information had been taken and destroyed—information she was the last to handle.

"I didn't do it," she murmured.

A shudder shook her from head to toe.

Several people had died. The responsible person would be charged with murder.

At least Tom was alive. Thoughts of her co-worker and boyfriend rose to the surface, but the memories felt numb, disconnected. Their relationship had been brief, a whirlwind of physical attraction. According to Brayer, he was on assignment in Bulgaria. She left him a message when she got back to the States, but he hadn't called.

"Where have you been?" Jake asked, watching her with a scrutiny that made her feel like she was beneath a microscope.

"Lost." The details of that day were foggy in Allie's mind. Flashes of memories and obscured dreams were all she had to piece together the events of that night.

Every bone in her body felt like lead. The energy—anger she felt fighting Johnny had flown the coop. She was tired—drained.

Her mom was dead.

Allie pushed out of Jake's arms. "Mom didn't believe Brayer Tech, did she?"

"No." He shook his head. "We didn't believe them."

"Please tell me this isn't true." Her plea was useless and she knew it.

Jake smoothed his knuckles across her cheek. "Honey, I wish I could. I loved Mabel like a mother."

Jake looked around the room that had once been bright and cheery, but now was weathered and worn like the rest of the house. "Mabel wouldn't let me help her. I tried." Mother like daughter, the woman was proud. On numerous occasions, he'd fixed things here and there for Mabel. Yet she wouldn't take money, nor any help beyond him fixing the occasional clogged toilet or sink.

Damn, he missed that woman.

When he lost his own mother three years ago, Mabel had been there for him. His father hadn't been. In fact, the SOB relocated to New York right after they laid his mother beneath the ground. Jake hadn't spoken to him since.

For a moment, it looked as if Allie couldn't speak. Finally she brought her misty eyes to meet his. "Did she suffer?"

Jake wanted to tell her how Mabel died with one of Allie's old letters in her hand, but the grief in her eyes made him hold back. Both he and Mabel had suffered from Allie's disappearance, but that didn't matter now.

"No. She just fell asleep and never woke up."

He knew there had to be a good reason for Allie not to have contacted her mother. Before Allie disappeared, Mabel received letters at least once a week when Allie was traveling and more frequently when she was stationary. Allie sent Mabel money when she could, but it wasn't enough.

A myriad of emotions played across Allie's face. "I missed her funeral." She gulped down big breaths of air. She gazed up at him with watery eyes. “Jake, I don’t understand what’s going on here. Who were those men carting Mom’s stuff away? And why?”

How was he supposed to tell Allie that he was selling some of her mother’s possessions? He’d arranged the sale a week ago.

Her sorrow was breaking his heart. He released a heavy breath. “Mr. Allen, Mabel’s lawyer, couldn’t find you. I had no idea how bad off Mabel had been financially. Her house was in foreclosure. She’d been making plans to go to a state subsidized home.” He had found her application lying on the coffee table in front of her the day he discovered her dead.

Allie wiped her eyes on the back of her hand. “Foreclosure? I sent money.”

He grabbed a couple tissues off the nightstand and pushed them into her hands. “It wasn’t enough. Last week the bank sold everything to the highest bidder.”

Allie’s head snapped up and she nailed him with a glare. “Highest bidder?” She wiped angrily at her tears and nose. He could almost see her reach for control as she straightened her backbone. “Who purchased *my* house?”

Allie wasn’t going to like what he had to say. “I did.”

“Thank God.” She swallowed hard, releasing a ragged breath. “What do I owe you?”

Owe? Her question caught him off guard. “Nothing.”

Her eyes widened. “Nothing?”

“The house isn’t for sale. I’ve already started moving in.”

Allie gazed up at Jake in disbelief. For a moment, she took in the man before her. This wasn’t the Jake O’Malley she remembered teasing and playing with as a child. When she’d left he had been a tall, lanky geek with glasses. Standing before her was anything but an awkward youth.

No glasses. His black hair was longer than the crew cut he wore as a young boy. It was still short on the sides, but longer on top. Silky tresses fell across one of his golden eyes. As if he knew what she was thinking, he brushed his hair out of his face. Spicy aftershave tickled her nose. She raised her head, sliding her gaze along a chest carved with lean muscle that stretched the red T-shirt he wore.

No, he wasn't the same boy she'd known. Nothing was the same anymore.

Allie pushed away from the bed and stood. Without a single word, she turned and walked through the open bedroom door. Heavy footsteps followed in her wake.

"Where do you think you're going?" Jake asked, hot on her trail.

"To my room," she replied, making her way down the hall. All she wanted to do was crawl into bed, sleep, and forget. Figuring out who owned what could wait till the morning. She opened the door to the bedroom she had grown up in and memories swept before her face in fast motion.

She was five. Life hadn't been easy, but her mom had always made it fun. She could see the two of them sitting in the middle of the floor, a map spread out before them as they chose where they would go to tonight in their dreams. Then the recollection was gone and she was eleven.

Milk—cookies. Jake beside her as her mother turned the pages in the encyclopedia, reading facts about Africa aloud. They were going on a safari. Once again, the memory faded and she was fifteen, braces on her teeth.

She was alone, hands tucked behind her head as she lay on her bed and stared up at the ceiling. *I'll leave this place one day*, she swore.

Allie blinked and she was back to here and now. She gazed around the small room.

It wasn't the typical little girl's room. There weren't any frills and lacy curtains. Like her mother, Allie had always dreamed of traveling, of seeing the world. Posters of faraway places adorned her walls. A large, colorful globe stood in the same place it had been for as long as she could remember, in front of her window. Rolled maps lay across her desk. Nothing had changed, except now her mother was gone.

She was just about to close the door, when Jake jerked it to a stop. "Uh. Allie. This isn't your room anymore. You're welcome to stay until you find another place to live."

This can't be happening.

"I'm too tired to argue with you. Go away." Allie didn't know what she had expected, but his insistence that this was his house wasn't what she'd anticipated.

Sympathy softened his eyes, but still he said, "Mabel is gone. This is my house."

For a second she thought of explaining her absence. Suddenly something burst inside her. She could feel every muscle and tendon snap. She curled her fingers into fists and lunged for the door. As she made contact, she thought, *I don't owe you anything.*

Allie didn't know what came over her. "The hell it is." The door flew forward, almost catching Jake in the face. He stopped it an inch before it struck his nose. He yanked it wide, the inertia throwing her forward and into his arms.

As their bodies pressed against each other, she released all the tension locked inside her. She kicked, screamed and flung her fists, until finally the tears came and she melted in his arms.

Perhaps the real reason behind her sudden anger was she had no place to go. This home was all she knew—all she had left of her mother. Allie didn't expect Jake to understand.

"She's gone, Jake. She's really gone."

In the middle of the bedroom where they used to play as children, Jake held Allie while she sobbed, choking sounds. She shook as if any minute she would fall apart.

He buried his nose into the scent of lilies lingering in her hair. He had always thought Allie and Mabel had a great relationship. He wouldn't believe that Allie would desert her mother to go God knew where this past year.

There were so many unanswered questions.

Jake stroked Allie's hair and held her close. "Hush, honey, it'll be okay." What the fuck was he saying? It wasn't going to be okay.

This was his home.

Mabel was gone.

He had sunk every penny he had into buying this house. He only had a small savings left from the stucco business he had started two years ago. If he stretched his dollars any further he'd put both home and business in jeopardy.

"I never got to say good-bye." Allie sniffled. "I wasn't here for her." She pushed away from him, and he let her go. Her forehead wrinkled as big tears swelled. The muscles in her jaws tensed as she fought to gain control.

He slid a finger beneath her chin and raised her gaze to his. "Where have you been?"

Tears spiked her long eyelashes. “It’s a long story.” She took a step backward, turning so that her back faced him as she walked to the globe before the window. She gave it a spin as a tremor shook her body. “Lost, Jake. I’ve been so lost.”

Chapter Three

The wind blew, whistling through the tree branches and tossing back Jake's hair as he kneeled in a puddle of mud. The water main in the backyard had busted just as he reached the front door. He had heard the loud pop and the rush of water as he turned the doorknob.

This was not what he needed. He had tons of work to do and wanted it finished before the storm hit.

Thunder rolled across the darkened sky as if threatening him. He only hoped the weather held until he finished fixing the leak.

One thing was on his side—if he hadn't come home from work to check on Allie his whole backyard would have become a swimming pool.

A twist of his wrist and the pipe cutter sliced through the PVC pipe. The break in the line shouldn't have been a surprise. The plumbing was old. Hell, everything was old and needed to be repaired. The house was literally falling down around him. Yesterday it had been a loose rail in the banister upstairs. He had to remember to fix it before someone got hurt. Today the water main—tomorrow?

"What the hell have you gotten yourself into?" he muttered, a frigid breeze cutting through his clothing as if he were naked instead of wearing his white coveralls and a long sleeve undershirt.

Grabbing an old rag from his pants pocket, he wiped moisture off the PVC pipe he held in one hand, then swirled some purple primer on the end. He waited a moment for it to dry before adding the adhesive and applying the sleeve where the break had occurred. As he held the pieces together, he gazed up at Allie's bedroom window.

It was Wednesday. For three days, Allie had locked herself in her room. She hadn't eaten a bite. Each time he had offered her something, she had turned him away. She didn't want to talk or argue, which really concerned him. He was worried about her. She couldn't go on this way.

He tightened the lids on both the primer and glue and pushed to his feet. "Tonight, sweetheart. Then I'll force feed you if I have to." Knowing she slept several feet down the hall from him was hard. Knowing she suffered alone was even harder.

The air was nippy, chilling him where his wet and muddy coveralls touched bare skin. Goose bumps raced up his legs, skittering across his arms. He looked down at his boots and clothes and frowned. "I can't go back to work like this. I'll freeze my ass off."

Quick steps carried him through the backyard where the gas and water lines flowed into the house. As he turned the main water line back on, he scraped his knuckles against the gas fitting. "Sonofabitch."

He shook his hand, easing the ache as he climbed to his feet and headed for the backdoor. Before he set foot on the porch, he scrubbed the soles of his boots on the grass, removing as much of the muck as he could. Slipping his boots off, he placed them beside an old, broken flowerpot. The cold from the cement porch radiated through his socks straight to his bones.

The screen door squeaked as he opened it and then pushed open the inner door and stepped inside. Warm air immediately surrounded him, as well as silence.

The morning dishes sat in the kitchen sink. Allie's plate full of eggs, bacon and toast lay untouched on the table.

He shook his head. "Dammit, Allie." The desire to force her into compliance was strong. His dominant nature threatened to take control, but now was not the time. Allie was hurting. She needed time to grieve.

The thought made him angry as he walked out of the kitchen into the living room. All he had ever wanted was Allie to return home. Now with her mother gone, there was no reason for her to stick around. Too soon, she would be out of his life again.

He wanted to go immediately to Allie, but he pushed the urge aside. He needed a shower and clean clothes. A quick peek to make sure she was all right before he had to get back to work.

Without hesitating, he headed for the stairs and the hall bathroom. He preferred taking a shower in this particular one for no other reason than it was the one he had used when he stayed over to look after Mabel, and the master bedroom's bathroom only had a bathtub.

Carefully he stripped out of his clothing, making sure no mud marked the linoleum floor. There was no time to shower and dress, much less mop the floor. Hell, he shouldn't have even left the job site, but thoughts of Allie were driving him crazy. If only she'd talk to him. He'd even take a smartass remark or two.

As he stepped into the shower stall, his foot slipped. His arms flailed as he grabbed the towel bar and caught himself before he went down. The floor was wet, slick with shampoo. The scent of lilies rose.

Had Allie taken a shower?

Just the thought of her naked, her hands moving slowly across her body, cupping her large breasts, gave him an instant hard-on. In fact, his dick sprang forth, eager for attention.

The breath he held eased out. Between the image of Allie and the drawing sensation in his groin, blood coursed his veins, filling his testicles to a tight and pleasant ache.

Simultaneously, he turned the hot and cold faucets on, finding just the right temperature. In no time, steamy water pelted his chest and ran down his body to swirl and disappear beyond the drain.

It felt good. It would feel even better if Allie was in front of him, pressed against his flesh as he parted her thighs and rode her hard. The image of her wet and aroused, her head tossed back in ecstasy as water sluiced over her skin made him one horny sonofabitch.

From the liquid soap container against the wall he squirted a dab of soap into his palm, rubbed his hands together and cupped his balls. They were hard and sensitive as he washed and fondled them, making his cock yearn for the same.

More thoughts of Allie forced his legs wide, shoulder-width. Without hesitation, he took himself in hand. What he really wanted was Allie's small hand caressing him. Instead, he tightened his fingers around his shaft. Slow, measured pumps from the base to tip as he drew a picture of her in his mind, an image of how she would look handcuffed to his bed, the fire in her gaze that he knew burned in her soul.

Jake closed his eyes and let his vision go. He could see her naked, sprawled upon his bed, a hunger for only him simmering in the depths of her blue eyes.

He didn't think it was possible but his cock grew firmer. A pang of sensation drew his balls close to his body and caused his grip and rhythm to increase.

Harder and faster, he thrust his hips forward, pushing his engorged erection through his fingers. With each stroke he visualized how it would feel to take her, mark her as his.

Would she fight him when he demanded she kneel before him? She would look so sexy, her hands shackled behind her as she took him into her beautiful mouth and sucked his cock.

"Fuck," he growled, riding the bittersweet edge of arousal.

The humid water beating upon him was a poor substitute for the caress of her tongue, the warmth and moisture of her mouth.

Jake groaned with the need to climax, holding back, not wanting the picture in his mind to vanish of Allie down on her knees, his erection slipping in and out of her lips. He leaned his free hand against the wall and threw back his head as fire licked his sensitive organ.

"Allie," he moaned her name just as hot rays of awareness shot down his cock, ripping a strangled cry from his lips. His climax hit with a force that rocked him back on his heels. A tremor raced up his spine. His hand shook, as he continued to pump his palm up and down, spilling his semen on the shower floor.

Heart pounding, he watched the remaining evidence of his ejaculation mingle with the water and wash down the drain.

"Dammit, Allie. What spell do you have on me?" Time and time again, he had tried to erase her from his memory, to forget the woman, but she refused to release him. Maybe if he fucked her he could get her out of his system. He could only hope.

Finishing up in the shower, he pulled a towel off the rack, and wrapped it around his waist. He stepped out of the bathroom, stopping short when he almost ran into Allie.

"Oh, my." Her eyes grew big as saucers as her gaze roamed up his wet body. Color spread across her cheeks, making him smile.

Was this the first time he had ever seen her blush? She looked simply adorable.

"Feeling better?" he asked, threading his fingers through his wet hair.

The fact that she was out of her bedroom was a good sign. Her eyes were red and puffy, no makeup, but her long wheaten hair was brushed, and she was dressed. Small toes peeked out from beneath her white jogging pants. A dark blue shirt was beneath the matching jacket she wore.

"Better?" she huffed, even as she did a double take across his bare chest, stroking his abdomen with her gaze as thoroughly as if her palms smoothed across his skin. His spent cock found new life. "Do you always walk around the house half dressed?"

Apparently, her spirit had returned.

"No, I prefer being naked." He started to unfurl the towel around his waist, wondering what her reaction would be if he let it drop.

Before he could release it, she croaked, "You wouldn't dare."

Oh, wouldn't I?

Holding the towel loosely around him, he headed toward his bedroom. Just before he reached the door, he let the towel slip from around his hips.

Allie gasped.

A chuckle tickled his throat.

Allie's heart jumped. She almost swallowed her tongue as she watched Jake's naked ass disappear behind her mother's bedroom door.

"I can't believe you did that," she sputtered in disbelief, but felt a slight grin overtake the frown she thought would never go away.

The boy she knew was gone—really gone—judging by the bulge between his legs that she'd noticed under the towel.

In his place was a man definitely drool-worthy. In fact, the transformation was quite astonishing. Even his stride spoke of confidence, arrogance, with a tinge of mischief. Neither had she missed the gleam in his eyes when he turned away from her. Nor the flush of heat that spread across her body like a thief stealing her breath. It had been a long time since she'd felt the touch of a man, even longer since she'd been laid.

Warmth singed her cheeks. Old familiar sensations assaulted her. Allie's pulse sped. Her nipples tightened to hard peaks and moisture dampened her panties. She bit her bottom lip.

Definite signs of arousal.

More than excited, she was horny.

The realization made her eyes widen. "Now is not the time for sexual ideas about Jake O'Malley. Sheesh." She pushed her breath out between clenched teeth. "You've known him all your life."

Even as she chastised herself, she wondered what those firm ass-cheeks would feel like beneath her palms as he drove in and out of her pussy. A flush of heat spread across her body with thoughts of his naked form pressed tightly to hers. His voice was deeper, sexier. Could he make her come with mere words?

"Oh God." She swallowed hard, butterflies flip-flopping in her belly.

It had been too long since she'd taken care of her body's demands. What she needed was a pair of strong arms wrapped around her. She needed to chase away the fact that she hadn't been here for her mother.

The muscles in her gut twisted with guilt. She hadn't told her mother how much she loved her. Allie's remorse was a douse of cold water over the warmth that had begun to flow through her veins.

Her gaze lingered on Jake's bedroom door. A rumbling in her stomach made her gather her thoughts. She hadn't eaten for days—hadn't wanted to.

The news of her mother had wiped Allie out, leaving her with a loneliness that went on without end. She'd gone through the shock and disbelief stages. The prescription medication the doctor had given her for headaches when Brayer's doctors had examined her had been a godsend. Between bouts of crying and screaming, she had slept most of the time. Her dreams were haunted with memories of her mom and the mysteries left unrevealed from her time in the jungle.

Each night she dreamed of the attack. Flames flickering toward the sky and smoke so thick she couldn't breathe.

But there was more—so much more.

A sense of danger that jerked her from sleep, soaked in perspiration, her pulse racing with fear. Sights and sounds that appeared so real they paralyzed her, until she woke to realize where she was. Each episode left her perched on the edge of remembering what happened, but her recall remained elusive.

Her mind felt so disjointed, like an electrical cord not completely plugged into a socket. Currents of memory flashed, then just as quickly disappeared. It was like chasing a mouse she had no hope of catching.

A heavy sigh released some of the weariness inside her. "Nothing will ever be the same."

Her feet felt weighted as she moved toward the top of the stairs. Since the news of her mother, a dull sensation had settled inside her. Even walking downstairs seemed like a monumental task instead of the familiar path she had bounded down repeatedly in her youth.

She raised her foot and was just about to descend the stairs when Jake appeared beside her. This time dressed in white coveralls, a dark, long-sleeve shirt, and boots. He gazed upon her with so much concern in his eyes that a tight pressure built in her chest. Without a word, he looped his arm around her shoulders and guided her downward.

"Are you hungry?" He gave her a squeeze.

"A little." She couldn't help leaning into the protective shelter of his body, noticing how right it felt to be near him, or how arousing his spicy aftershave smelled as it enveloped her.

For over a year, all she had smelled in the jungle was decay, mold and body odor, including hers. She wouldn't even think about the long hair on her legs and armpits. Allie chastised herself because that wasn't a fair assessment of the Amazon. When she had first arrived, the rainforest had held her in awe. Sweet-smelling, vibrant orchids of purple, yellow and white, and lilies with elongated, papery, arrow-shaped leaves joined a variety of other beautiful flowers and ferns that grew on the ground or sprung from the green canopy of trees and vines overhead. The exotic plant life was a romantic's paradise with foliage like the hot lips plant—so-called for its similarity to a certain part of a female's anatomy. Some varieties even looked like a pair of red-hot lips.

"I got your favorite." Jake's voice jerked Allie back from her wanderings. The expression of pride on his face chased away the concern that had been there earlier.

"My favorite?" She never realized how sensuous his eyes were, liquid gold, hot enough to stoke the small flame that sparked behind the shadows inside her. Maybe in his youth his black-rimmed glasses hid their beauty. She stole another look.

Yep. They were eyes a woman could drown in all the way to heaven.

Side by side, they took each step. His muscular body rubbed against hers, causing her nipples to ache and a wave of uncontrollable desire to leak between her thighs. Allie decided that friction was a bad thing when it had been over a year since she'd had sex. She held her breath, releasing it when they were finally standing on the living room floor.

His arm slipped from around her shoulders to grasp her hand. She immediately noted how big and strong his fingers felt closing around her smaller ones.

"Yeah. Your favorite. Bologna, pickles, and potato chips. Come on. I have fresh bread, too." As he pulled her toward the kitchen, the telephone began to ring.

"Hold on." He released her and backtracked to the telephone at the bottom of the stairs. "Hello, O'Malley's residence. Yes, she is."

Allie frowned with the reference, but it disappeared when the hand he held the receiver in jutted out toward her. "It's for you."

"Me?" A couple of steps had her standing before him. A slight ache throbbed in her arm as she took the receiver from his hand. The doctor who had examined her when she arrived in the States was amazed at the fantastic job the Machiguengas tribe's medicine man had done setting her broken arm. Straight as a needle, but she stilled suffered a dull pain now and again. Allie pressed the telephone to her ear. "Hello."

There was dead silence on the other end.

"Hello," she repeated.

Click. The steady buzz of a dial tone greeted her.

"It's dead." She raised her gaze to meet Jake's curious stare.

"Probably just a bad connection." He took the telephone from her and hung it up, before he gathered her hand in his. "Let's eat." He playfully wagged his brows. The roguish grin he gave her warmed her body and made her pulse speed as he led her to the kitchen.

A sense of relief filled Allie as he released her hand and headed for the refrigerator. She needed time to get her raging hormones restrained.

He motioned to table. "Sit down, and I'll make you a sandwich."

She drifted down into a chair before the table and watched as Jake went to work in the kitchen. He moved in tight, controlled steps, poised and confident. What was more disturbing was that he knew where the plates and silverware were. Every stride revealed he was at home.

His home—not hers.

Allie felt tears touch her eyes, but she fought them back. This wasn't right. None of this was right. Her mother should be alive. This was her home.

A wave of anger rose so quickly it startled her. It swarmed around her like a red cloud to heat her cheeks and sting her eyes.

Anger at her mother for leaving her.

Anger at Jake for taking away her home.

Anger for the time lost in the jungle.

And anger at herself for not being there for her mother.

She pushed away from the table and stood. "I'm not hungry." An empty hollow feeling slammed into her stomach along with a soft buzz in her head. She swayed and the room spun. Allie grasped the table to steady herself.

Wearing an expression of concern, Jake set the mayonnaise jar on the counter. "Sit, before you fall."

She snapped her hot glare at him, daring him to make her. Yet she doubted she had the wherewithal, feeling like she currently was. The room still swam before her.

As he approached, he said, "Allie, honey. Sit." He lowered his voice as if he were speaking to a child. "You have to eat something."

She squeezed her eyes shut and fought to gain her composure. When she opened them again, everything was as it should be. Nothing moved that shouldn't.

"Dammit, Jake, this is my house." She swung her arms wildly to encompass the area around her. "My house, my kitchen. *Mine-mine-mine.*"

My mother, she silently cried, now sounding like a child. But she couldn't help it. She was losing everything that meant anything to her. Allie swallowed the lump in her throat, looking at him through misty eyes. *Please Jake. Don't take my memories away from me.*

He never said a word, only took the necessary steps to close the distance between them. She tried to jerk away, but he captured her in his arms.

"Let me go," she choked, holding onto the last thread of control. Yet, as he folded his arms around her, she disintegrated into a ball of tears.

She didn't know how long she cried, or when Jake picked her up in his arms, sitting at the kitchen table to cradle her against his chest. Her emotions felt like she was riding a seesaw, up one minute—down the next. She closed her eyes, releasing a heavy sigh.

What a mess.

Tenderly, he pressed his lips to her forehead. "You okay?"

She nodded, inhaling his masculinity before she said, "We need to talk."

With short, quick movements, he moved her off his lap and onto another chair before he stood. He ignored her as he grabbed a loaf of bread, opened it, and pulled out several pieces to place upon two plates. The knife he picked up clinked against the mayonnaise jar as he began to coat the bread with dressing.

"Jake?" Allie wasn't the type of person to let things lie. They needed to work through this issue with the house.

"First you eat." Piling potato chips and pickles atop a piece of bologna and bread, he completed making the sandwiches by topping them with another slice of bread and then squishing the sandwiches together. He placed one in front of her, the other across from her. Quickly, he walked toward the refrigerator, opened it and grabbed a gallon of milk. After pouring two big glasses, he sat down facing her.

"Eat." He picked up his sandwich and took a bite. She followed suit.

The salty-sour flavor of the potato chips and pickles was heavenly against her palate. “Mmmm...” She closed her eyes, savoring the taste. “I haven’t had one of these in years. Thank you.”

Forgetting herself, Allie smiled. She had missed so much of her old life. Milk, being one of them. The glass was cold to the touch as she picked it up and took a sip. The chilly liquid flowed down her throat, coating and easing the turmoil in her stomach. After she set down the glass, Jake reached across the table and wiped her milk mustache away. The tenderness of his caress made her feel weepy. “Jake—”

As if he knew what she was going to address, he said, “Now’s not the time, Allie.” He crammed the last bite of his sandwich into his mouth, and downed the rest of his milk, before he pushed from the table and rose. “I’ve got to get back to work before the storm hits.”

“When?” Allie didn’t like loose ends, and her life had been one long loose end this last year.

“Later.” Heavy strides carried him toward the living room.

Before she could move away from the table, she heard the door slam shut.

Chapter Four

Twilight was closing in on Jake, the orange and red hues of the setting sun barely visible in the west as he steered his truck into his driveway. He seldom used his garage, preferring to park his truck outside. Turning the key, he cut the engine and sat there for a while just staring at Allie's window on the top floor.

It had been a hell of a day—a long one too.

Not to mention, last night he'd been awakened by someone trying to break into the house through the arcadia doors in the kitchen. He'd checked on the disturbance, but no one was there. Pry marks, scrapes on the metal, on the outside of the door, evidence that it wasn't his imagination. It was probably a bunch of damn teenagers thinking the house remained vacant. The house had been unoccupied for two weeks after Mabel's funeral. Teenagers were always looking for an abandoned place to hang out.

Still, unease robbed him of what was left of the night and his sleep.

A heavy breath pushed from his chest.

There had been no time to stop for lunch, no time to check on Allie as he had yesterday. He had hoped her appearance, the fact that she had showered and eaten, marked a turning point. Yet before he left to return to work, she had disappeared once again into her bedroom. She hadn't come down for supper or breakfast this morning.

He opened the truck door and got out, slamming the door before he headed toward the front door of his house.

How much longer would she grieve alone? Didn't Allie know that she could lean on him?

He stepped on the porch and began stomping the dirt from his boots when he abruptly stopped, foot suspended midair. A sliver of panic rushed to his heart as he slowly settled his foot on the concrete.

Something was wrong.

The rotten egg stench that slapped him in the face, burning his nose and making his eyes water, was the first indicator of danger. The next was an unusual noise, a hissing or more accurately, a roaring sound that came from around the side of the house.

Gas. Judging by the strength of the odor twisting his stomach into one giant knot there was lots of it.

Without a second thought, he threw open the front door. It sprung wide, bouncing off the wall. He cringed, waiting to see if anything would happen.

The slightest spark—and boom!

It made his gut churn to think of what that stupid move could have cost him.

Allie.

She was alone.

The situation was volatile. He had to move quickly, but cautiously.

God, he refused to think of the possibility.

At the top of his lungs, Jake yelled, "Allie!"

His feet nearly flew beneath him as he sped through the house and up the stairs. Reaching the top, he hit the hallway running. Just as he reached her bedroom door, she opened it.

Rubbing her eyes, she grumbled sleepily, "What's the matter?"

There was no time to explain. Gas needed little reason to ignite. A flick of a light switch or the vibration of a telephone ringing could cause the house to burst into a ball of flames. He had seen the effects on a job site one summer. A backhoe the landscaper was using had hit a gas line. A nearby welder's torch had set the home ablaze, killing several people and leaving a hole in the ground where the house once stood.

Even now, the offensive smell was making its way through his house. It was less obvious upstairs, but it wouldn't take long to engulf the entire place.

Jake grabbed Allie by the arm and started pulling her down the hallway. She jerked her arm, planting her feet, but he didn't release her. Instead, her bare feet slid across the wood flooring, making a squeaky sound.

"What the hell is going on?" Her concern now turned to anger. She pinned him with a hot glare.

As they stumbled down the stairs, he muttered, "Gas leak."

Recognition dawned in her eyes, widening them. "Oh my God."

She covered her nose with her palm, the odor growing more obvious with each step. Suddenly, her resistance flew out the window, her steps now in unison with his as they made their way to the front door.

They both crashed through the entrance, coughing, only to inhale more gas deep into their lungs. They didn't stop running until they stood across the street. Only then did Jake yank his cell phone out of his pocket and dial 9-1-1.

"What is your emergency?" the female operator asked.

"Gas leak," he answered, sweeping his gaze over Allie. She wore only a black T-shirt that barely covered her ass, her long legs exposed to the light breeze that chilled the night. She stood with her arms wrapped around her. An expression of trepidation twisted her pretty features as she stared at the house.

Even dressed in his coveralls, he felt the night air. She had to be freezing.

"Sir, is everyone out of the house?" the young woman on the telephone line asked.

"Yes," he responded, wanting to go to Allie and warm her.

"Please verify your address." The operator continued to hammer him with one question after another, before she said, "Mr. O'Malley, help is en route." Even as she spoke the words, he could hear sirens in the distance.

Jake snapped his cell phone closed and moved closer to Allie. He pulled her into his embrace, rubbing his body against hers to keep her warm. She willingly wrapped her arms around him. Already her nose was turning red, her skin frigid to the touch.

The first to arrive was a police officer who parked several houses down the street and made his way to them on foot. Quickly on his heels were a fire truck and another patrol car. The gas company was only seconds behind the rest of the emergency vehicles. In tandem, they worked to secure the area and address the issue. Carefully, they tracked across his lawn and disappeared around the house.

In no time, the residents of the neighborhood began to swarm the street. Curiosity seekers were held back a safe distance by the police. The occupants of the homes to the right and left of Jake's house, as well as the one that abutted his backyard on the next street, were evacuated.

Ms. Tatum, who lived kitty-corner and across the street, approached with a wooly blanket in hand. She gave Jake a concerned glance, before she focused her arthritic eyes on Allie. "Come here, child."

Jake released Allie, and she stepped toward the thin, elderly woman who draped the throw around Allie's shoulders, covering her completely.

Allie tugged the blanket tightly around her neck. "Thank you, Ms. Tatum."

"You're welcome, dear." The silver-haired woman gave Allie a hug. "Sorry about your mother. She was a good woman. I'll miss her."

Allie's chin quivered, but she held on to her control. "Thank you."

"It's so good to have you home. How are you faring?" Ms. Tatum continued to probe.

Tears welled in Allie's eyes. Jake could almost see her resolve starting to break, but she held off her emotion.

"Ms. Tatum," he interrupted. "Thank you for the blanket. I was wondering if you might have a cup of coffee to warm Allie?"

"Oh my goodness. Yes. Why don't both of you come in out of the cold and we'll talk about your mother." Jake saw Allie swallow hard at Ms. Tatum's invitation.

"Thank you. I think both of us are too concerned to leave. But the coffee would be appreciated and maybe a pair of slippers," he quickly added, looking down at Allie's bare feet.

A sigh of relief made Allie's shoulders rise and fall. "Thank you," she whispered for his ears only. "I can't talk about Mom. Not now."

Jake pulled her back into his arms. "I know, honey."

They had time to have two cups of coffee before someone from the gas company finally came over to speak to them.

A man in his late thirties brushed back his sandy hair. The patch on his uniform revealed his name was Bob. "Damn lucky you are. For now we've pinched the line and turned off the valve to the entire neighborhood. You'll need to get this fixed asap. It's not unusual for pipes to corrode, but—" Something close to suspicion lit his eyes. "I see a water line was fixed recently." He narrowed his gaze on Jake. "You been messing with the gas lines too?"

"Me?" Jake's voice rose defensively. "Hell, no. Why?"

"The fitting looked tampered with. Wrench marks. But the leak happened down the line—looked like it had been punctured."

What Bob implied was devastating, not to mention it made absolutely no sense. Who would want to do something so dangerous?

"Maybe I accidentally struck it with the shovel when I fixed the water line," Jake offered.

Bob raised a skeptical brow. "No, these were wrench impressions. Could you have mistaken the water and gas lines, then realized your mistake?"

Jake crossed his arms. "I know the difference between a gas and water line." He didn't even try to restrain the anger in his voice.

Bob had the nerve to give him a *yeah-right-buddy* look. "Maybe it was kids playing a prank. It's happened before. Kids have no idea of the danger." He looked at Jake appraisingly. "Problems with anyone lately?"

Dammit. Jake recalled last night's attempted break-in. Anxiety crawled beneath his skin.

"The house is being aired out. All windows open and fans on. Harder to ventilate on cold nights like tonight," Bob explained. "As soon as the levels are safe, you and your neighbors can return to your homes."

ജ്ജ

Allie was freaking freezing.

After almost three hours, the officials finally let everyone return to their homes. The gas had dissipated, but the pungent odor of rotten eggs lingered. Jake had explained that gas was odorless; the obnoxious smell was an additive so that people could detect leaks.

She stepped into the living room, her feet frozen, almost numb in the thin slippers Ms. Tatum had loaned her. The moccasin-looking house shoes were damp as she pulled them off. In seconds, her toes began to thaw and then throb.

She hated being cold.

Jake began to build a fire in the hearth. She moved to the couch and sat down, Ms. Tatum's blanket pulled tightly around her.

"It'll be warmer in a minute." Jake worked efficiently, using kindling to start the fire, and applying several logs of wood when the flame was established.

Luck had been on their side. The hearth had only cold ashes. The fire Jake had built earlier that morning had died out before the gas leak.

His dark hair was mussed, white flakes of stucco caking it, as well as his coveralls. Even his handsome features were marred with the white chalk.

Jake had always been conscientious. Whether it was his job down at the local grocery store or school, he was governed by his scruples. Although he owned his current stucco company, it was apparent he labored alongside his men.

He was a hard worker—a good man.

The ring of the telephones, one sitting on the end table next to the couch, the other on a small table next to the staircase, made her startle.

"Get that will you?" Jake asked, stoking the fire.

She reached for the telephone, the blanket around her slipping off her shoulders. "Hello." The moment was awkward, should she say, "Grant's residence" or "O'Malley's"?

"Alison. Is that you, baby?" A smile crept across her face as Tom rambled on. "I can't believe it. I heard what happened. Damn, I wish I'd known."

"Tom." Her throat squeezed, making her voice hitch. From the corner of her eye, she saw Jake snap his head around. She felt the heat of his gaze.

"Yeah. It's me, baby."

"Where are you?" Tears beat at the back of her eyelids.

"In Bulgaria. I just got your message. I'm sorry I wasn't there to protect you."

Allie struggled to hold onto her control. Swore she wouldn't cry. "How long will you be there?"

A crackle in the phone line made her press the receiver closer to her ear.

"What?" Tom's voice sounded hollow, far away.

"When will you return to the States?" Her hand clenched the phone as she raised her voice.

"Probably will be at least a year." The cracking sound in the reception grew louder. She struggled to hear him. "Do you remember anything about that night?"

"Not enough to make any sense. But more is coming to me." It wasn't a lie. Her dream last night had revealed a faceless assailant, one who chased her through the jungle. She ran barefoot, as always in her dream, her feet cut and bleeding.

The static in the line grew thicker, drowning out his next words. She barely caught, "Gotta go—" before the line went dead. The dial tone blaring in her ear made her head begin to throb. Her hand shook as she put the receiver back in its cradle. With a tug, she pulled the blanket around her shoulders.

"Who was that?" Jake rose from his stooped position. He brushed his hands on his coveralls, little pieces of stucco falling on the carpet.

"Tom," she muttered, finally feeling the warmth of the fire penetrating her.

"Your boyfriend?" A note of something close to bitterness rang in his voice.

"Yes. Well—" Could she call someone she had only known for a short time and apparently wouldn't see for a year or longer a boyfriend? A guy who appeared to easily move on with his life without a blink of an eye? "No, not really. A friend. Tom's just a friend."

"I'm going upstairs," Jake grumbled, sounding like a big grizzly bear. He barely made it to the stairs when the telephone rang again. This time he answered the telephone closest to him. "O'Malley's residence." There was a slight pause, before his gaze shot to her. "Yeah. She's here." Jake let his arm and the telephone he held fall to his side. "It's for you."

"Me?" Since she'd returned to town, Allie hadn't contacted any of her old friends. She hadn't wanted to see or speak to anyone. She hadn't even left the house, even to visit her mother's grave. Visiting it would be accepting a reality she wasn't ready to face.

Jake nodded, bringing her attention back to the phone. The only people who would be contacting her would be work-related, and she wasn't sure that was a good thing. The last time she had spoken to Brayer Tech was with a host of investigators. They grilled her for several days. Insisted she meet with their doctors, before releasing her and allowing her to come home. Oh, and there was that reminder not to leave the country.

Once again, she reached for the telephone on the end table beside the couch were she sat. As she did, Jake hung up the one he held. "Hello."

"Alison." A familiar male voice she couldn't quite identify came over the receiver.

"Yes, this is Alison." Allie watched Jake take the steps two at a time, until he disappeared from sight.

"Todd Granger here." Her boss at Brayer Tech sounded a little unfriendly, definitely not the pleasant man who had hired her.

And why would he be calling so late at night? It was almost ten o'clock.

"We need to talk." He sounded unsettled. "Where the hell have you been?" he barked. Before she could respond, he continued. "Do you have any idea how this makes me look?"

"You?" The chill was completely gone from her body. Instead, anger lit a flame beneath her. "Exactly what are you saying?"

"Your disappearance doesn't look good on either of us."

Allie saw red, flashes of the jungle popped in and out of her mind's eye. "You sonofabitch," she snapped. "I don't give a flying fig how it looks. You're not the one who lost a year of your life. You're not the one with nightmares, memory loss."

The other end of the telephone went quiet for longer than was comfortable. "There's a lot of angry people, researchers who have devoted years of their lives, not to mention the investors who have sunk millions of dollars into this project. Did you know they were close to a breakthrough?"

A breakthrough?

That's why Darrel Mendel had insisted she work into the night transcribing all the scientists' notes. She remembered his excitement. The campsite had been abuzz.

"Listen, Todd, I'll say this only once. I had nothing to do with destroying or stealing information." Allie was at her wit's end.

"But you were the last one to handle the data. You were supposed to make backups. This is your fault. Someone has to pay."

Allie's head began to pound even harder. This was a nightmare. Evidently, no one believed she was innocent. "I made backups," she almost screamed into the telephone. But what good were backups when they were ravaged by fire?

"I can't stand beside you. I won't go down with you." Panic rang in his voice.

What exactly was Todd saying?

"You're on your own, Alison." A click sounded in her ear. The conversation had ended.

Allie buried her face into the palms of her hands. She needed a lawyer.

Chapter Five

Friday night everything about Allie said she was aching for a fight. The scowl she wore added to the worry wrinkles pressing into her forehead. Her movements were quick and sharp as she paced the floor, only stopping to flip the sleeve of his jacket lying across the couch. Guess he was lucky she didn't toss his coat on the floor and stomp up and down on it.

From the second the door closed behind him, she had moved like a caged tigress—restless—walking a path in the already worn carpet of the living room. Fact was she'd been like this ever since the gas leak incident night before last.

Through the split in the black robe she wore, he caught a glimpse of her thigh.

What did she wear beneath the flimsy silk robe?

A fire blazed in the fireplace, casting shadows. As if the room needed any more heat than what this particular woman already generated. Wind whistled through the chimney, stirring the flames. Orange and red sparks sputtered from the hearth.

As Jake unlaced his boots, he watched Allie make another tour around the room. She stopped and glared at everything that belonged to him. First was a piece of Western art hanging where a picture of an old English cottage use to be, then his coat rack, and finally his shoes from last night. Each time she passed one of the items, she made low grating sounds.

Stuffing his socks into his boots, Jake remembered he'd seen Allie in a similar tirade before, but somehow this one seemed more formidable. She was putting all her pain and guilt behind it. The best thing for him to do was to march up those stairs and ignore her.

Boots in his hands, he made for the stairs.

"Where are you going?" she barked.

Jake clenched his teeth and tried to remind himself that she was grieving. Anger was one of the steps toward healing.

He'd been there—done that.

There were many times he had wished to go off on someone, but didn't. Fact was there was no one else for her to take it out on except for him.

He reached the first step before he turned around and replied, "Upstairs. Shower."

Allie flapped her arms like a bird taking flight and made a discouraging huff. "Sure. Make yourself at home."

He took a deep breath. *Patience. She's hurting.* He started back up the stairs.

"But it isn't," she bit out sharply.

Midway up the stairs, he paused and once again turned toward her. "Isn't what?"

Fists propped against her hips, she haughtily raised a brow. "Your home."

He was exhausted, too tired to argue with her. The rain had interfered with finishing the home he had promised would be completed today. The customer had said she understood, but he hated falling through on a promise. He was a man of his word.

For a second, he listened to the splatter of raindrops pelting the windows. Darkness had fallen early. He prayed his crew retrieved all their equipment and they'd made it safely home.

And now there was Allie to deal with.

The little spitfire stood at the bottom of the stairs, aching for a fight. Her eyes sparkled with fury.

Just ignore her. He shook his head and continued up the stairs. "Not tonight, Allie." The patter of heated footsteps followed.

"Don't walk away from me," she huffed from behind him.

He didn't stop until he was in his bedroom. Neither did Allie as she swung open the door he had closed. It hit the back of the wall with a bang.

Great. Just one more thing to fix.

She stood in the middle of his room glaring at him. Even as he shrugged his arms out of the straps of his coveralls and jerked his shirt off, baring his chest, she remained apparently unmoved. That is if the fire in her eyes was any indication.

As he undid the buttons on the side of his coveralls and began to drag them to his hips, she stuttered, "W-what are you doing?"

"Undressing," he responded.

Color dotted her cheeks as her eyes widened. "Here?"

He glanced around the room. "Uh. Yeah. Bedroom."

She pinched her lips together. "You don't scare me."

His undressing wasn't meant to scare her. He only wanted a warm shower, something to eat, and the comfort of his bed. "Fine." He dropped his pants around his ankles, baring the white briefs he wore.

When his thumbs slipped beneath the elastic band of his briefs, she cried, "Jake." Her voice was shrill. "You wouldn't."

"Look, Allie, we've played this game before. You know I will. So either stand there or get out of my room."

She steeled her shoulders, giving them a little shake that said, "Go ahead."

His briefs fell around his ankles and he stepped out of them.

The muscles in her throat tightened as she swallowed. With just a grin, he dared her to look away.

Instead, she nailed her gaze right on his hips, making his body's temperature soar. All thoughts of exhaustion and needing a shower flew out the window. His cock jerked alive, lengthening and arching toward his belly button.

"Come here." The timber in his voice deepened. Man, he wanted to hold her in arms.

Nervously, she wet her lips. "Not interested." She raised her eyes to meet his. If he wasn't mistaken, the fire burning in her gaze wasn't fury any more, but arousal.

Jake took a step forward. "Liar."

Her body swayed as if to move away from him, but she stood firm.

He took another step toward her. "If those perky nipples pressing against your robe are any indication, I'd say you're very interested."

Allie snorted. "In your dreams, buddy."

Another step brought him closer, until he stood directly in front of her. He leaned down, bringing their faces within an inch of each other.

"Kiss me," he whispered. She smelled of lilies and soap and a night filled with pleasure.

Their gazes locked in a mental battle.

"Never," she snarled. Her chin tilted arrogantly.

His nose lightly touched hers. He caressed her softly, urging her to close the distance between their lips. “Kiss me.”

He heard the ragged breath she sucked into her lungs. “No.”

Slipping a palm to the nape of her neck, he felt her silky tresses against the back of his hand. “Kiss me.” As he applied pressure, she stiffened, resisting him.

Fine. Now wasn’t the time. She would come to him sooner or later.

Jake released Allie and stepped backward. Without a word, he walked past her, out of the bedroom and into the hall bathroom. He pushed the door closed. Leaning against the cool wood, he glanced down at his engorged erection.

“Looks like another hand job, buddy.”

After stepping into the shower, Jake twisted the faucets to start the water. Temperature regulated, he allowed the steamy water to wash over his tired muscles.

Damn, but he was tired, add to that horny and he was in a difficult position.

He raised his face to the flow of water, which suddenly turned icy cold.

“Shit,” he shouted, jumping from the shower, dripping water all over the floor as he grabbed a towel. His once hearty cock died a fast death, shriveling close to the shelter of his body. “*Arghhh...*” He shivered, wrapping the towel around his shoulders.

Safely outside the shower, he stood twisting the cold water completely off. Scalding hot water met his touch. “Sonofabitch.” He jerked his hand back. “What the hell is going on now?” As he turned the faucets off, the soft tinkling of laughter sounded from behind the closed door.

"Allie!" he yelled.

Crap. Allie hightailed it toward her bedroom, shutting the door just before Jake burst from the bathroom.

The pounding on her bedroom door startled her, but she didn't move.

"You little witch. Open this door." Jake didn't sound too happy.

"Serves you right," she shouted at the closed door. The pipes in the house had always been a little finicky. She had learned that much as a child. Too many times, she had begun to bathe just as her mother started the dishes. The result was hot or cold water—never anything in between.

Truth was she could use a cold shower about now. It had taken all her strength not to accept what Jake offered, a night in his arms. Even now, her body burned with need.

Allie's heart raced as she leaned against the locked door. From the other side, Jake shook it so that she felt the tremor clear to her bones.

"Allie, let me in," he growled.

"Beat all you want. You're not getting in here." Vibrations from his pounding continued to shake the door. Abruptly, they stopped. Allie harrumphed. "Giving up so soon?" A chuckle of satisfaction rose and died as quickly.

She shouldn't have taken her temper out on Jake. Everything that had happened recently was overwhelming. She was in trouble—big trouble.

Jake had been good to her mother—good to her. He didn't have to let her stay here. Truth was this wasn't her house. But that hadn't stopped her from making an appointment to meet with her mother's lawyer tomorrow.

The click of the lock sent her into action. "Oh, shit!" Allie flung herself against the door, but it was too late. Jake rushed through still only wearing the towel low around his hips. The inertia sent her backward and she fell on her ass. Pain radiated up her spine.

"Sonofabitch!" *That hurts.*

Before she could rise on her own, Jake yanked her to her feet, firmly against his solid chest. The lines on his face were hardened, but his eyes were not.

Damn man was enjoying himself. Her anger flared anew, racing like a wildfire across her cheeks.

He gave her a little shake. "I ought to jerk you across my lap and beat your ass."

She glared at him. "You wouldn't dare."

Jake released her, except for the iron grip he had on her right arm. "The hell you say." He began to drag her toward the bed.

Planting her heels into the worn carpet, she balled her freed fist and swung.

With lightning speed, he caught the punch and slammed her back against the wall. The air in her lungs gushed out on impact. She recovered quickly, countering with a raised knee to his groin that missed its mark. Just in time, he swung away only returning to pin her flat against the wall with his unyielding body.

Trapped. She couldn't move—couldn't breathe, except for the spicy, masculine scent that assailed her.

Damn. He was good. He knew her way too well, anticipating every defensive move she made.

"Release me or I'll—"

In a surprise response, he stole her threat away with a punishing kiss.

There was no gentleness in his touch. Teeth meshed with teeth. His invasion was demanding, forceful, as his tongue pushed past her tight lips. Fast and skillfully, he tasted every inch of her mouth.

Her struggles for release were futile. He was bigger—stronger—and his body covered hers like a shield.

This definitely wasn't the boy she knew.

Allie whimpered, caught between anger and the slow burn he stirred inside her as he ground his hips to hers. His arousal pressed tight against her belly. His masterful kiss plucked the strings of her desire, pulling her deeper and deeper under his control.

But he wouldn't win, she swore to herself, even when his warm hand slid between the folds of her silky robe. Yet when his fingertips worked past her camisole to cup her breast, she silently screamed, *No! You won't win—*

Her breath caught as he squeezed her nipple.

Sweet pain splintered through her breast as he increased the pressure. The radiating sensation filtered through her globe, heading down south to tighten low in her belly.

Anger and need collided, releasing a fresh wave of desire between her thighs.

It had been forever since she'd made love, felt her body satisfied.

The truth was she needed to be held. With everything that had happened, Allie needed a strong man's arms around her more than anything.

Before Allie could change her mind, she wadded her hands in the towel around his waist and pulled. The deep rumble in his throat only heated her blood more. Her fingertips weaved through his light dusting of chest hair. Within seconds, he had her devoid of her robe, camisole, and panties, her heavy breasts against his moist chest.

For a moment, he didn't speak and only stared at her breasts. The desire in his eyes stoked the fire inside her.

Again, he captured her lips in a fiery kiss, hungry and fierce. He smoothed his palms slowly up the outside of her thighs, then moved inward. She inched her legs apart, waiting breathlessly as he skimmed closer to her pussy.

A deep growl vibrated next to her neck sending a shiver through her.

His fingers played across her skin. Every place he touched sparked with life.

His gaze was hot—sultry.

She released a squeal as he pushed her back against the cool, stucco wall and lifted her off her feet.

"Wrap your legs around my waist." His voice was a dark seduction, so demanding.

She locked her ankles behind his waist, pressing his erection hard against her wet folds. Before she could weave her arms around his neck, he captured both wrists in one large hand and held them high above her head. He looped his other arm beneath her ass. His body did the rest to keep her suspended.

"Jake—"

She tried to suck in a much-needed breath, but he took that moment to shift his hips and drive his cock deep inside her.

"*Ahhh...*" she groaned. Jake was so large it took a moment for her body to soften and receive him. When he moved deeper, filling her completely, all thought, not to mention argument, fled from her mind. Her only coherent reflection was how wonderful he felt buried inside her. Then he began to thrust, not gently, but hard and fast.

Oh God. It was heavenly.

Allie had never had a man fit her so perfectly—one who made her pussy hum as he did, moving in and out of her body. Every muscle tightened with delight, every nerve ending came alive.

Stinging rays shot up her chamber. "Jake!" she screamed, writhing against him. Hands pinned above her head, she jerked for release, but it was useless.

He slammed into her body with a force she felt at the back of her womb. Her orgasm moved closer and closer. She needed what lingered just out of reach, driving her insane, as her breasts rasped against his chest.

"Come for me," he rumbled.

With a twist, he ground his hips to hers, doing a little movement that blew the head right off of her control. Those three little words and the heat behind them lit her fuse. She shattered into a million pieces of sensation. Warmth flared across her body. A light sheen of perspiration glistened on her skin. Her inner muscles contracted. White-hot beams of fire coursed through her. She threw back her head, hitting it against the wall as she cried out in ecstasy.

A shiver wracked his body as he continued to pump inside her hard and fast. He leaned his forehead on her shoulder. She knew he rode the razor edge of his climax by the tension in his body.

"Allie," he roared, as he buried himself one last time between her thighs and froze. In a gush, she felt his warm seed release. His cock jerked several times and then stilled.

Both breathing hard, they remained locked together. The moment was surreal, filling her with the only peace she had felt in the last year. Until he released her arms and let her feet touch the floor.

"Fuck," he muttered in a tone of regret. He moved away quickly, as if she were diseased.

The immediate sense of emptiness swamped her. His magnificent cock was still semi-hard, jutting from a dark nest of curls.

Her gaze caressed a path across his billowy chest, taut abs to his eyes. He was frowning. For some odd reason he looked angry.

The answer came to her like a slap to the forehead.

Condom.

This wasn't Jake's brightest move. Sex without a condom only complicated things. "Honey, please tell me you're on the pill."

She gave him a *duh* expression. "Jungle. Lost. Remember?"

Well, that answered that. He couldn't allow Allie to leave now, not before he determined if she carried his baby. The woman had a habit of disappearing.

Jake pushed his fingers through his hair as he moved away from Allie. He took a moment to ease the pounding in his chest, but all he could think of was taking her again.

She looked confused, hurt. As he reached for her, she dodged his grasp. Her breasts rose and fell with her rapid breathing as she looked aimlessly around.

What had he done?

It started out as paybacks for the cold and hot water during his shower, quickly escalating to his need to kiss her. All he had meant to do was tempt and tease her. Make her want him as he had wanted her all these years.

When she ripped the towel from around his waist, he had lost control. Fact was he never had any control when it came to Allie. He had dreamed of fucking her since he was in high school. Even then he knew she would be uninhibited, wild.

Alison Grant was the kind of woman who always went for what she wanted.

For once, Jake wanted to go after what he dreamed of—Allie. He wanted to be the man she surrendered to night after night, even if in reality it was for one night.

Hands shaking, she knelt to retrieve her robe.

The musky scent of sex permeated the air making his cock lengthen. It jerked, drawing her attention.

Confusion turned to anger, as she appeared to get a second wind. Her hot gaze stroked him, as her tongue swiped across her lips. "This is just great." She pushed her arms through the robe and fastened the sash around her waist.

Jake reached out for her again. "Honey—"

"Don't honey me." There was a sexy little growl in her voice. Her fingers curled into fists. Her body trembled with her fury.

Allie was magnificent when she was angry. He could almost feel her energy crackle in the air.

Her eyes closed. She pressed a palm to her mouth. "What am I going to do now?" Her tone softened. She sounded almost lost.

"Wait," he offered. There wasn't anything else they could do.

Her eyes flew open. "Wait!" With fast strides, she began to pace the small confines of the room. She stopped once, opened her mouth and then snapped it closed. A couple more turns around the room and she faced him. "This won't happen again."

He folded his arms over his chest. Let her think what she wanted, because Jake had no plans of ever letting her go—ever.

As if she could read his mind, she stated emphatically, "It won't, Jake."

Was she trying to convince him or herself?

She nailed him with a scowl. "Are you leaving?"

Clearly, she wanted him gone. Jake knew there was nothing he could say to change her mind, so he made his way to the door. Before he passed through it, he faced her. "Allie, this isn't over." He shut the door behind him before she could respond.

Chapter Six

Early Saturday morning light shone through a slit in the drapes, which meant Jake hadn't slept for more than four hours. In a daze, he stumbled toward the master bathroom. Cool air caressed his nakedness. He opened the door, shuffled in, and blinked when he switched on the light. While he relieved himself, he shook his head, trying to chase his sleepiness away.

The night hadn't ended quite like he had hoped. Once again, he and Allie were at odds.

The toilet made a swishing sound as he flushed. Listlessly, he stood for a moment listening to the swirling water before he moved away and turned the faucet on. Cold water rushed over his hands, the shock waking him a little more. He yawned, turning the faucet off and reaching for a towel.

Nothing he could do about Allie until morning. He just hoped she was in a better frame of mind, open to the possibilities of what lay before them—a future relationship. Pushing his fingers through his hair, he released a heavy sigh. He leaned against the sink and stared into the mirror.

Dammit! Dreams of waking with her in his arms had haunted him for so long. He'd been so close. Now they had to worry about the possibility of her being pregnant. Strangely, for some reason he couldn't quite feel guilty.

He could be a daddy. A hint of a smile rose.

Jake wanted Allie—always had—and he'd take her any way he could have her.

As he headed back to bed, his feet seem to take on a mind of their own, heading toward the hallway. He braced his hands against the doorjamb, refusing to take another step.

Just one peek, his subconscious urged. *You know you want to.*

That's when an unfamiliar noise caught his attention.

Crying.

God, he hated to know Allie was hurting. He followed the soft weeping, which became louder as he descended the stairs to the living room.

A soft glow flickered in the fireplace throwing shadows across Allie as she sat bundled up in her mother's old recliner. It swayed gently, as she whimpered.

He took a step to close the distance between them. "Allie?"

"Go away, Jake," she breathed through her tears.

Jake knelt at her feet, placing his palms on her thighs. "Let me help you."

She wiped furiously at her tears. "Help? Can you bring my mother back?" she lashed out. "Or my memory?"

"No—" His brows pulled inwardly. "Memory?"

What the hell was she talking about?

"Forget it. Go back to bed." She buried her face into the lightweight quilt that used to lay at the foot of her bed, until Mabel brought it downstairs. Mabel had worn it around her shoulders as she rocked, telling him once that it made her feel closer to Allie.

He sat quietly at her feet, fingering the frilled edges of the quilt. "Your mom told me you two made this."

An uneasy huff sounded beneath the cover. Her muffled voice rose as she said, "It was a Junior High project that would have blown up in my face if it hadn't been for Mom." Slowly, she lowered the blanket so her reddened eyes appeared. She sniffled. "My sewing skills sucked, but Mom loved this old quilt." She batted away the last of the tears that spiked her eyelashes. "She laid it at the foot of my bed, so every night I'd be reminded that together we could accomplish anything." Her chin quivered as new tears slid down her cheeks. "She's gone, Jake."

He settled on his knees and wrapped his arms around her shoulders. "I know, honey." The quilt fell away and he saw she was wearing the same lacy camisole she'd been wearing earlier. Her full breasts pressed against the soft material. A stirring began in his groin, but he pushed his wayward thoughts away.

"I didn't get to say good-bye." Her body shook. "I didn't—" she swallowed hard, "—tell her I loved her."

Jake stood, sliding his hands under Allie and lifting her so that he could slip beneath her to hold her in his lap. Her lacy panties slid up to bare an ass cheek. "She knew, Allie." He pulled her closer to his chest, covering the quilt over both of them. "You're all she ever talked about." He began to rock her gently.

Allie drew her knees to her chest, burrowing next to his body. "She must have been so lonely, scared, not hearing from me."

He brushed a lock of Allie's hair from her tear-stained face. There wasn't any reason to tell her Mabel had suffered greatly. Night after night, he had sat with Mabel while she fretted over her daughter. "Where have you been?"

"Peru, in the Pongo area."

He knew that much from what Mabel had told him. "No. I mean this past year."

She looked up at him with so much pain in her eyes. "It's like a piece of my life has been erased." She shook her head as if she couldn't believe her own words. "All I remember was working late one night. Something was about to break—a discovery the researchers and scientists were working on—everyone worked late that night." She went quiet. "Then nothing..."

Her pause unsettled him.

"The next thing I knew I was in the belly of the rainforest and the newest member of the Machiguengas. Believe me, that was an experience." Uneasy laughter bubbled in her throat. "I couldn't understand them. They couldn't understand me. Time is elusive when your memory is gone. I made marks on a piece of wood each day. Sixty-two was the count, before I remembered who I was. I don't know how many days or weeks I was unconscious before I started counting." The forlorn look on her face was heartbreaking. "You have no idea how scary it is to not know who you are." Her voice sounded brittle.

Again, she grew silent.

Jake was stunned speechless. The image of Allie frightened and alone made his throat tighten.

"A group of missionaries came to the village. If it wasn't for them, I'd still be there."

Jake didn't know what to say. Instead, he rubbed his cheek against hers wanting in some small way to let her know he cared—that she wasn't alone. She felt so soft beneath his touch. The sparks in the fireplace crackled, catching his gaze, but not his attention.

"What happened to you?"

She shrugged. “I don’t know. I have sketchy memories—dreams that I can’t tell if they’re real or my imagination. From what the missionaries could extract from Kuru, the tribe’s chief, they found me in the water, unconscious. Washed ashore, I guess. They cared for me until I was able to take care of myself.”

Jake shuddered to think how lucky Allie had been. The Amazon itself was host to a variety of wild animals, including jaguars and ocelots, the river filled with anacondas, not to mention piranhas.

He felt the shuddering sigh that coursed through her, before she gazed up at him with sorrow in her eyes.

“Months went by. I didn’t think I’d ever make it back home, much less civilization.”

A flood of empathy assailed him; despair, anguish, and anger for all she went through alone. He drew her closer, holding her tighter.

“After I arrived at the U.S. Embassy I called the pharmaceutical company I worked for. Someone had sabotaged the campsite—everything destroyed—years of research.” She licked her lips. “I’m their prime suspect.” Again, she shook her head in disbelief. “There are a lot of upset people, my boss, the scientists, the investors. Hell, the villagers and save-the-rainforest activists didn’t even want us there. They found my hut burned to the ground like several others. They searched the jungle, but found nothing—including me.” Her chin quivered as if she fought to control her emotions. "I don’t know whether there are other suspects or other people missing from that night. The company said very little, keeping the details tight-lipped.”

Jake’s warm embrace felt good. Allie knew she should move away, but no way could she leave the comfort of his arms. She needed to feel safe. Lord knew her nights were filled with broken memories and a sense of panic that made her heart race and always woke her covered in sweat.

After her telephone calls with Tom and her boss, her nightmares were becoming more vivid—more desperate. Throughout the night, she had awakened swinging her arms frantically, fighting faceless demons and gasping for air.

Even during her waking moments, she had begun imagining the screech of parrots, the mournful cries of a jaguar, and the chatter of monkeys. At different times she could smell the scents of the jungle, stagnant water, decaying vegetation, the air so heavy that it pressed on her chest like a vise.

The memories made her inhale deeply, but instead of the rancid smells she was familiar with, she breathed in Jake's masculine fragrance, spicy and warm. Safe. She couldn't help snuggling closer.

Gently, his palms moved across her bare skin, so different from their previous encounter. He had touched her with domination, taken her hard and fast. And she had loved every minute of it.

"What do you remember?" he asked.

Remember? She recalled everything, except what would free her from the panic and fear that had become her life.

Allie zoned out, visualizing tall columns of gray and brown trees, some covered in white patches of lichen. Broad branches large enough they could be respectable sized trees, extended out from the trunks to create the canopy above. Countless hues of green light filtered through the foliage. But at night, very little moonlight seeped in.

Buttress roots snaked across the forest floor, but it was a knotted liana, a tropical woody plant, that had caught her foot. She'd tripped, struggling desperately to rise.

"Running." As she said the single word, her pulse began to race. "I was barefoot. My feet hurt. Branches cut into my skin." Screams of the villagers and screeches from animals high above her filled her ears. "Someone was chasing me."

Dammit. She hated how the memories made her feel—afraid. Even now the bitter taste of fear was on her tongue.

Her heart pounded as she continued. "Fire reaching toward the darkened sky. The smell of smoke. I couldn't breathe." She felt cold, unable to get enough of Jake's body heat as she wrapped her arms around him. "Then nothing. Nothing..."

Jake rocked her, gently rubbing her back as he tried to console her. "Shhh...honey, it's okay."

Allie pushed away from him and looked him square in the eyes. "No, Jake. It will never be okay. Not until I can remember what happened that night. I'm innocent. I know I am."

He leaned forward and brushed his lips softly across hers. It wasn't a sensual kiss, but one filled with compassion and caring. It made tears burn behind her eyelids.

"Surely they don't believe you're to blame for the attack," he stated more as a fact then a question.

"The company had their doctor examine me. Guess they didn't believe my amnesia story. The physician said my physical injuries weren't to blame for my loss of memory." She reached up and touched the back of her head where it had healed, but left a ragged scar she could feel.

As he pushed her back so that their gazes met, she could see concern darken his eyes. "Injuries?"

"Head wound." She shrugged. "Broken arm. More importantly, the doctor explained something traumatic must have happened during the attack on our campsite that I'm refusing to remember."

Lord knows she had tried to remember the events of that night until wracked with pain—her head hurt so badly that aspirin did no good in relieving the ache. The investigators had seen the results after hours of questioning her. She had required sedation, losing another day in getting home. It appeared that no one believed she was innocent. What the hell was she going to do?

"I might never learn what happened in the Amazon." She couldn't stand the thought of not knowing why a part of her life was lost. Not knowing why someone was chasing her or how she ended up buried deep in the jungle.

Every tense muscle inside her stretched tight. So much had happened in the last couple of weeks. Her body and mind felt stressed to the limit. If only she could sleep without the dreams, and now she had to add the loss of her mother and the guilt building with each second that ticked.

Jake pulled her against his chest. "You're home now."

"Home? Like you said, 'This isn't my home, not anymore.'" Allie couldn't help the bitterness filling her voice.

Jake winced just before he stood, cradling her in his arms. "Let's not discuss that now." Without another word, he moved toward the banister. She hugged his neck, holding onto him as he climbed the stairs and reached the landing. Barefoot, he padded down the hallway.

Using his hip, he pushed her bedroom door wide and strolled toward the bed. Gently, he laid her down, slipping in beside her before he jerked the blankets over them.

Allie should have stopped him from pulling her into his arms, but she didn't have it in her. No way did she want to spend the rest of the night alone. Instead, she nestled nearer, burying her face against his chest, as her palm smoothed across his bare hip to his back. He drew her closer, tucking her head beneath his chin and throwing a leg across hers.

Even though his erection pressed firmly into her belly, he made no advances. He held her as if he would never let her go.

Sleep tugged at her eyelids, drawing them down upon her cheeks. Allie fell asleep wrapped in Jake's embrace.

Jake lay awake for what seemed like forever, holding Allie. Her sleep was restless as if she fought demons. She cried out several times, the pitiful sounds wrapping around his heart and squeezing. Once he wiped away tears that welled beneath her closed eyelids. Allie had gone through hell only to return home to find her mother dead and her house lost to her.

"What am I supposed to do?" he whispered.

Jake loved Allie, but he wasn't a fool. She didn't care for him the same way. She had left years ago without a goodbye. Truth was she was a vagabond at heart, wanting to see the world. As hard as it was to see her suffer, Jake knew he had to look out for himself. This was his house now, and although he planned to do everything within his power to keep her here, he had to prepare himself for the reality that she might leave again.

Tomorrow he would begin moving the rest of his stuff in. He had no alternative. The lease on his apartment would soon expire and he'd have nowhere else to live. Allie would just have to understand. At least that's what he told himself as he kissed her softly on the forehead and drifted into sleep.

Chapter Seven

Allie jerked awake to what sounded like machine gun fire, a loud bang that repeated over and over. Her mind felt hazy, almost as if it were cotton. She closed her eyes. "It isn't real." The vibration shaking the walls wasn't her imagination. The sudden crash of something shattering yanked her into a sitting position.

"Holy shit!" It sounded like the house was falling apart.

She swung her feet over the edge of the bed, jumped up, and raced to the door. Flinging it open, she headed down the hallway. More banging told her it was coming from her mom's room.

Allie skidded to a stop just inside the bedroom. Every one of her mother's possessions was gone. In their place was an enormous four-poster bed, nightstands on each side, a large masculine dresser, an armless rocking chair and a footstool. The smell of new furniture and lemon oil filled the room.

Two men on ladders were hanging a full size mirror on the ceiling. When they caught sight of her, smiles slid across their faces.

Crap! She was still wearing her skimpy lacy camisole and matching panties—no robe.

Being caught half-undressed was nothing compared to what she saw next. Jake strolled past her carrying a handcrafted wooden box. As he set it upon the floor, the lid bounced open. He wiped his hands on his blue cotton shirt, giving her a wicked grin as he moved his jeans-clad legs shoulder-width apart.

Wide-eyed, she stared. The contents stole her breath.

Toys. Sex toys.

Several of the items she recognized, others she didn't. Right on top was the biggest dildo she had ever seen.

Her gaze snapped to the mirror on the ceiling then back to the chest. What kind of kinky crap was Jake into?

"W-what's going on here?" she stuttered. Her shocked gaze darted from Jake to the large dildo and back. "Where are my mom's things?"

Jake snapped the lid to the box shut before the men on the ladders could see what it held. "I rented a storage facility. I thought you might want to keep her bed and dresser. The rest I had boxed for you."

Jesus help her. Jake was erasing her mother's presence. Gone was the scent of roses. Gone were all the trinkets she'd given her mother throughout the years.

Allie couldn't help it. She trembled with fury. "I want all of her things carted right back in here—now."

"No can do. Remember this is my house—my room." Jake glanced toward his box of toys. "Don't touch any of those things," he said, moving past her and through the open door leading into the hallway. His boots tapped across the floor.

She spun on the ball of her foot, following Jake. As they reached the stairs, she said, "You can't do this." Her voice was thick with desperation.

He didn't even turn around as he strolled down the stairs. "Allie, please."

"But-But—" She almost slipped on the newly polished steps, catching herself by grabbing onto the banister before she fell on her ass.

Reaching the bottom of the stairs, he pivoted, and she almost ran into him. "Stay as long as you want. But you're going to have to accept that this is my house now." He began to move through the living room and straight for the open door leading outside.

Allie knew he was right, but—

She picked up the pace and continued to follow him. "Dammit, Jake." She stopped, her fists perched on her hips. "Don't make me take you to court, because I will."

"Do what you feel you have to," he slung over his shoulder, as he pushed through the front door and walked outside.

"Ohhh..." she cried, as she ran after him.

This wasn't looking good—not at all.

Allie wanted to scream with frustration when the two men from the bedroom appeared.

"Mr. O'Malley, we've finished. Is there anything else you want us to do?" the shorter of the two men asked, as the other went to a beat-up Ford pickup and placed his toolbox in it.

Jake picked up another large box out of the bed of his lipstick-red, jacked-up Chevy truck and set it on the ground. "No. That should do it. Thanks, guys."

The serviceman handed Jake a clipboard, he took a moment to sign off on the order and then handed it back. Retrieving his box, Jake headed for the door.

The anxiety in Allie's body soared as she followed him through the living room and back upstairs toward her mother's room.

She was speechless.

He was stealing her house, but more than that, her memories. Slowly, her mother was fading from sight and it tore her up inside to admit it.

"Jake, please." She hated the whine in her voice. He had her by the short hairs.

He set the box on the floor of the bedroom and turned to her. "I'm sorry if this is bothering you. I only have a couple of days to move out of my old apartment and into here."

"It's a waste of time. You'll only have to move everything back out. I'm seeing Mom's lawyer today."

His features hardened this time with her threat. He glared at her before reaching in the box and retrieving several large odd shaped metal rings attached to metal plates and a handful of screws. Silently, he went to one of the ladders and carried it to the corner where her mother's curio cabinet had stood. He offered no response. Instead, he picked up an electrical drill and climbed the steps.

Within seconds, the room filled with the grind of the hand tool as he placed several of the metal plates in a triangular pattern into the ceiling. Drywall dust filled the air.

She gasped, inhaling the chalky substance, as he continued to deface her mother's room. "What are you doing?"

The roguish grin he gave her didn't warm the cockles of her heart. "They're D-rings. Hand me those chains out of that box."

For whatever reason she did as he requested, standing on tiptoes to hand them to him. He looped one chain through a D-ring, and then another chain to the one D-ring adjacent to it. The D-ring closest to the wall he strung both chains through so that they hung to the side. Carefully, he stepped from the ladder. He tapped his knuckles several places against the stucco wall until he found a stud. The drill roared to life. Again, drywall dust spewed into the air as the bit chewed through the wall. The hollow whine the drill made said he missed the two by four. He attached the D-ring into the wall anyway. "I'll redo this one later. For now it'll have to do."

He stepped past her and began to rummage through the box until he found two parachute locks, which he snapped onto a link of each chain securing them to the D-ring on the wall. Again, he went back to the box, extracted two smaller hooks and two baskets of vinery, attaching both to the ends of the chains hanging from the ceiling.

It looked quite nice, and Allie felt a little bit of her anxiety slip. That was until he stooped to his knees and started drilling into her mother's wood flooring.

Her eyes widened. Her mouth gaped. "Oh, my God. You're ruining the floor. Stop!"

He ignored her, continuing to attach two more D-rings to the surface.

The smell of wood shavings made her even more desperate to stop him. "Jake, please."

The drill droned, falling silent as he turned it off. Still on his knees, he glanced up at her with real concern in his eyes. "Allie, I can only imagine how hard this is for you. Honey, I'm sorry, but this isn't your house anymore."

He switched the drill on. It hummed loudly, but died a quick death. Several times, he played with the switch clicking it off then on, before his gaze followed the cord to the end where the plug dangled in her hand.

Jake jumped to his feet and before she knew it, he locked his arms around her. *Damn. He was fast.*

"You want to play, honey?" His whisper was low and deadly, sending a shiver up her spine. She knew fighting him was futile—she'd already tried that once. Instead, she glared at him.

Like that was going to work.

One hand locked securely around her back, he used his free hand to push a strap of her camisole down. He kissed her neck as he dragged the other strap off her shoulder. She felt the lacy material start to slip down her breasts, stopping just before baring her nipples.

Lust burned in his eyes as he caressed her bare skin with his gaze and then licked the same path his eyes had made. The touch of his warm, wet tongue made her skin prickle. "Maybe I'll show you exactly what those D-rings are for."

With his fingertips, he skimmed lightly across her flesh, dipping into her cleavage to pull the camisole further down to expose both nipples. The minute the cool air hit them they puckered into tight peaks. A tremor shook her to her core.

"Jake—"

He placed a finger against her lips. His eyes darkened, as his voice deepened. "Allie, have you ever been tied to a bed and fucked?"

For a moment, nothing really registered except the fact that Jake wanted to have his way with her. She replayed his words in her mind, focusing now on the "tied to a bed" part.

Holy shit! Jake was into bondage and domination.

Oh, yeah. She'd read about people like him. A thrill of excitement rushed through her, even as embarrassment heated her cheeks. If she had to admit it, the whole idea of being bound and fucked intrigued her—always had, but she'd never had an interested partner.

"I can tell by the fire burning in your eyes you have or at least have thought about it. I bet you'd enjoy me running a flogger across your tight ass." He wet his lips, drawing her attention to his mouth. "Or maybe even being spanked." He gave her a playful whack on the ass that did two things.

It made her scream out in surprise and her ass cheek sting. Oddly, the strange sensation felt oh-so-good. Even to the point of washing away some of her anger and replacing it with a hint of desire.

Focus, Allie.

She couldn't lose control. This was her home. Now was not the time to be getting intimate, especially with Jake. Still, she couldn't help thinking about the large bed behind her or having her arms and legs strapped down while the man before her introduced her to a life she had only dreamed about.

"The fire in my eyes is the need to kick your kinky ass out of my mother's room."

Lie. Lie. Lie. Yes. She'd been inquisitive about bondage and domination when those shocking pictures had popped up on her computer screen late one night. When she'd mentioned them to Tom, he had stared at her as if she was nuts.

Damn, if those snapshots hadn't made her hot and envious of the woman whipped and taken by not one, but two men.

Now there was a fantasy. Multiple partners.

A sweltering expression slid across Jake's handsome face.

Crap! He saw right through her façade.

Using a single finger, he circled one of her nipples, teasing and plucking it until rays of sensation spread throughout her breast. A tightening feeling followed in her belly that dampened her panties.

He ground his hips to hers so that she felt his hardening erection. "If I stripped you naked and tied you to my bed, would you fight me?"

The glimmer in his eyes said he'd like that. The picture he drew in her mind kicked her arousal up a notch, but the increasing bulge in his jeans made it difficult to think. She sucked in a shaky breath. “Damn straight I would.”

Her words said one thing, her body another, when she didn’t step away from him.

At first, his caress was tender. Gently he rolled one of her sensitive nipples between his fingers, increasing the pressure little by little. She gasped at the pleasure-pain his touched induced, wondering how much she could take if he pinched harder.

“What if I handcuffed you to the chains hanging from the ceiling and secured your ankles to the floor, spreading you wide? Would that turn you on?” His voice was deep and sexy.

Just the image he painted in her mind released another rush of desire between her thighs. “I hardly think so,” she managed to say.

“What if I did this?” He leaned down, captured her nipple in his warm, wet mouth, and sucked long and hard. His mouth made a popping sound as he released her. “But with my lips wrapped around your clit, sucking the sweet thing into my mouth, sliding my tongue deep inside you to taste your hot cream?” He cupped her breast. “Honey, I’ll make you come like you’ve never done before.”

His naughty words sent a shiver up her spine. She squirmed against him, knowing that the wall she had erected was crumbling.

Crumbling? Jake’s words felt like a wrecking ball smashing into her. She was so friggin’ hot small tremors exploded in her womb like firecrackers, spasms of delight that tore away her anger and left her arousal burning out of control.

Her body tensed in his arms. She brought her hands up and fisted his shirt. She couldn’t take any more. Allie wanted this man.

"Shut up, Jake, and fuck me. Any way you want—just take me now." She pulled him to her and thrust her tongue between his lips.

She broke the caress to take a breath. His expression grew intense, eyes smoldering like pools of hot liquid gold.

"*Any* way?" The sultriness in his voice left her with only one response.

Not yes, but, "Hell, yes," she hissed, feeling the heat of his stare burn beneath her skin. If he wanted to tie her to the bed or chain her to the ceiling and floor, she was game and ready. Her body literally cried out to be caressed. Her nipples were tight nubs, breasts heavy with need, and her panties were now drenched with desire.

Besides, she knew that Jake would never hurt her. They had been friends too long. Strangely, she felt safe and horny, not a bad combination and not exactly how she had planned the day. But there was no way her body was willing to turn him down.

Shut up, Jake, and fuck me. Any way you want—just take me now. Allie's words rang in Jake's ears.

His heart beat a fast staccato as he moved away from her toward the handcrafted wooden box. He wasn't into the full-fledge BDSM scene. It wasn't a lifestyle he lived. Although the elements of bondage and toys and having a woman submit to his kinky tastes was fucking hot in the bedroom.

Blood rushed his cock and a pounding ache resulted.

Allie would look so sexy, naked and chained, or spread wide on his bed for his pleasure. Just the thought of delving between her thighs and tasting her hot moist cream on his tongue drove him past the point of no return.

God, he wanted Allie with a need that went beyond obsession.

His back to her, Jake bent and retrieved several items and then turned. From one finger, he dangled red fur-laced handcuffs, ankle bracelets and a collar. Each of the items had a much smaller D-ring attached to them with a spring lock.

Her eyelids popped open, but she didn't say a word. In fact, she licked her lips as if in anticipation.

Adrenaline burst through his veins, hot and wild. She was really going to allow him to chain her to the ceiling and floor. Blood gushed into his balls, hardening them and creating a sweet ache that made it difficult to move.

"Strip." His voice was hoarse, gravelly with need.

Allie's eyes brightened as she stared at the swinging manacles. She hesitated only a second. With quick, jerky movements, she pulled her camisole over her head and dropped it to the floor. She hooked her thumbs into the waistband of her panties, pushed them from her hips and down her legs, until she stood naked before him.

Eager. He liked that.

The sight before him sent his libido into overdrive. His cock throbbed, firming his balls past the point of comfort.

"Put your hands before you." He took the necessary steps to close the distance between them as her hands rose. With each step, his legs slid against his testicles, robbing him of breath. There was something about pleasure and pain he craved. He wasn't into sadomasochism, but he hungered for the point where pain became pleasure, intensifying the rush of an orgasm for him and his partner.

When he placed the first handcuff around her wrist, he felt the tremor that shook her. He couldn't help wondering what she was thinking as he handcuffed her other wrist. Did she feel him stripping her control away little by little? Did she crave it as much as he did?

A furry ankle bracelet in each hand, the collar dangling from one finger, he placed his palms on her waist. A slow cadence began as he caressed them down her hips, thighs and calves, loving the gooseflesh that rose in their path as he knelt. Within seconds, he snapped the separated cuffs around each ankle.

The curly little nest of hair in front of him was so inviting. He couldn't help himself. He leaned forward, pressing his nose to her mound and breathing in her female scent. She smelled sweet, with the heady aroma of her arousal making his cock harden more. He had to taste her. Bracing his hand on her thighs, he flattened his tongue and licked a path along her slit. She jerked, releasing a soft whimper. Her nectar beyond anything he had imagined. As he had promised her earlier, he wrapped his lips around her clit, sucking the sweet thing into his mouth, before sliding his tongue deep inside to taste her. She cried out, her hips pressing into him.

Jake ached to watch the flush of a climax wash over her, but that would have to wait. He was anxious to see how far she would let him go.

He released her and stood, taking several steps backward. His heart nearly stopped. "Beautiful. Even more beautiful than I have dreamed over the years—" The last word caught in his throat. He hadn't meant to speak out aloud.

The shocked expression on her face melted into a smile. "So you've thought of me while I was gone." Her eyes sparkled with the knowledge.

Well, hell. What was he suppose to say? That he saw her face in every woman's reflection? That every night he dreamed of holding her in his arms?

Nah...

Instead, he moved before her and fastened the collar around her neck. He hooked his finger through the D-ring and led her to where the two baskets of vinery hung. Removing each basket and setting them out of the way, he placed the spring lock of each handcuff to the dangling chains. Carefully, he adjusted the chains affixed to the wall so that her arms stretched tight above her head.

A thread of unease flickered in her eyes as he plugged in the drill. It hummed to life as he switched it on.

"Jake?" Her voice crackled. "I don't—"

"Relax, honey. I just need to finish securing the last D-ring to the floor." Relief softened her features.

After he was finished anchoring the D-ring, he said, "Spread your legs."

Her chest rose and fell, pushing her full breasts forward. She sucked in what looked like a breath of courage. A single step wedged her legs apart. The snap of the first lock securing her ankle startled her. She remained silent as the final click sounded.

Stepping away, he felt a wide grin force the corners of his mouth upward. Now this is exactly how he had dreamed of her the night before. Naked, her wrists and ankles manacled for his pleasure—and his pleasure was just what he was seeking.

Without a word, Jake strolled back to the box. Her eyes widened when she saw he held several whips. The black handles were leather wrapped, with multiple narrow strips that measured at least eighteen inches. One in each hand, he worked the floggers simultaneously so they hissed through the air.

He saw the first signs of regret heat her face. "I don't know about this, Jake." She wetted her lips.

He slowed the swing of the floggers until they lay quiet at his side. “I’d never hurt you, Allie. All you have to say is stop.”

He’d never force her to go beyond her limits or do something she wasn’t comfortable with. Still, he prayed she wouldn’t ask him to release her.

She swallowed hard.

Jake placed a finger beneath her chin, stared deep into her eyes. “Do you want to play with me, Allie?”

Chapter Eight

Play with him? Allie's body hummed with the need for Jake to play with her. *Damn you for being so sexy.* She stroked her gaze across his handsome features.

"Yes." She wanted this opportunity to experience something she had only wondered about.

His eyes glowed with approval. "Good."

Jake laid the whips on the bare mattress of his new bed and slowly began to undo his shirt. Each released button spread his shirt wider and wider, until he shrugged and it slipped from his shoulders, leaving her breathless with anticipation.

He was magnificent, from his sculptured biceps to his broad chest. She loved the way his chest hair circled his hard nipples. Her gaze followed the path of hair that swirled around his bellybutton before dipping beneath his jeans.

She licked her lips, unable to wait for the unveiling of his thick cock. He made no move toward removing his pants. Disappointment made her frown. Instead, he sat on the bed and pulled off one boot followed by the other. Each made a dull thud as they hit the floor. Ever so slowly, he removed his socks. Barefoot, he stood, gathering the two whips in his hands.

"What about your jeans?" she asked, looking at him through lowered lashes.

He raised a brow.

Allie could see the grin he fought to hide.

"Patience." Again, he worked the floggers through the air, building the tension of when those leathers straps would touch her skin. It was obvious that he knew how to wield the whips, as they moved artfully in unison, heating her blood.

Exactly what had Jake been up to while she was gone?

"Where did you learn such a skill?" she asked, mesmerized at the quick movements of the whips.

"I actually attended a class."

"You're kidding?" Her disbelief must have shown, because he laughed.

"Nope." He moved closer, his lips touching her ear as he whispered, "Learned all the sweet spots on a woman's body guaranteed to make her scream with ecstasy."

God, she was going to come with just the thought. Her nipples stung, little spasms sparked in her womb, and moisture built between her thighs.

When the cool thongs finally touched her skin, they were gentle, teasing and sliding across her shoulders, down her breasts. Her nipples knotted into aching nubs. He moved behind her and she felt the strands brush against her ass and thighs. Again, he dragged the whips across her ass, but this time several of the strands wedged between her butt cheeks, sending heat across her skin.

"Do you like that, honey?" he murmured against her cheek.

Her heart was pounding. The beats echoed in her head. "Yes."

He pressed his naked chest to hers. His jeans rasped her sensitive skin. "Would you like me to spread your cheeks and penetrate your ass with my cock?" Before she could answer, he stepped backward.

Oh, Lord. Warmth spread across her face, as her breath caught. She had never experienced *that* wicked pleasure before.

A single flogger snapped, biting into the tender flesh of her buttock. She yipped, a high-pitched sound of surprise. The sting was sharp and painful, but quickly dulled to heighten her arousal. Gently, he continued to tease her with the flogger, drawing it over her skin, then snapping it, sometimes lightly—sometimes not.

He stirred behind her and she felt his finger slip down the crease of her ass and spread her globes wide.

"I asked you a question, Allie." His voice was husky.

Her mouth parted, but before she could reply his warm, wet tongue traced the path of his finger.

She jerked against her restraints. "*Ohhh...*" she cried out, shocked at the intimacy of his touch. The gentle probing of his finger against the puckered skin made every muscle in her body stiffen. His fingertip threatened to push onward, pulsating lightly against her anus.

"Yes or no, Allie? Would you like for me to fuck your ass?" he asked, continuing to tease her.

"Yes. God, yes," she groaned, pushing back against his finger, waiting for the moment of penetration that didn't come. Instead, she felt the heat of his body disappear as he moved once more toward the chest on the floor.

A tingling sensation raced across her skin. What was he up to?

The devilish smile he gave her could not be good—or could it?

A whisper of concern filtered through her mind when he pulled a tube of lubricant and an odd-shaped glass object from the container. Her brows furrowed. She knew what that was.

Oh, my God, a butt plug. She had seen them advertised on an internet site she had visited one lonely night.

As he began to coat the bulb with lube, she knew exactly what he had in mind. It was an unconscious reflex. She clenched her ass-cheeks tight. Her anxiety level was clawing up her back.

"Jake?" The chains rattled as she shifted her feet as far as the restraints allowed, which wasn't much.

He strolled to her side and brushed his knuckles softly across her cheek. "Honey, do you want me to stop?"

Did she?

No matter what her mind was telling Allie, her body tightened in all the right spots screaming this is what she wanted. She was an adventurer. She sought new experiences. And she wanted to go where Jake offered to take her.

Allie sucked in a breath and shook her head.

"Good girl." The smile he gifted her with eased her somewhat, but when he moved behind her, she gripped the chains.

"Relax," he coaxed, placing lube at her entrance. Achingly slow, he began to apply pressure, but instead of the plug, his finger eased inside her. Fire exploded through her canal, startling a cry from her parted lips. Her body tensed. She fought her bindings.

He pressed his chest against her side, the feel of his jeans rough against her hip and leg. The warm scent of spice surrounded her. "Breathe. The burn will subside and the pleasure will be more intense. Trust me."

Breathe? It was more like short, quick pants.

"Slower." His finger buried deep inside her, he kissed her shoulder, playfully nipping the skin beneath his teeth. "Inhale deeper, release it slowly."

When the pain eased and her pulse calmed, he began to work his finger in and out of her taut entrance. Amazingly, the sensation went from a burn to pleasure. Never had she felt anything so raw and erotic. He dipped a second finger deep inside her, stretching and arousing her further, hot moisture dampened her thighs. Overpowered by the new sensations, she moaned softly.

"Like that, honey?" The sensuality in his voice stroked her as effectively as his finger.

"Yes." She choked on the answer.

"Are you ready for something bigger to slide in that tight, sweet hole?"

Oh, yeah! She nodded briskly.

Soft laughter greeted her eagerness.

His fingers slipped out of her ass, and then she felt the head of the butt plug probe and stop as it reached the taut ring of muscle, stretching it until the plug popped past it. Sharp, burning pain and then an incredible fullness filled her.

"Ohhh..." Her cry came out a strangled groan. Her ass tightened on the foreign object, causing her womb to clench and release. Her pussy pulsated with the need for attention, but instead he disappeared into the bathroom. She heard the water running. Then he returned, wiping his hands on a towel that he threw aside. In seconds, she felt threads of sensation explode against her ass as he once again struck her with the flogger.

She arched beneath the sweet pain quickly chased away by his touch as he stroked her skin and whispered, "You're beautiful. So pink and hot." His deep, seductive voice slid up her spine, making her tremble.

Allie had never felt anything so intense. He alternated from light, teasing strikes to sharp, stinging blows—ones that made her whimper and silently beg for more.

"Do you like it rough, honey?" His breathing was harsh, his mannerisms more anxious as he grabbed her ass, creating the sensation of a thousand needles pricking her flesh.

Working both of the whips again, he lashed her buttocks until the skin was tight, warm and tingling, paying special attention to the tender spot where her thighs and ass met. Just when she thought she couldn't take any more, he stopped.

Something thudded upon the floor, before she heard the whisper of his zipper falling, the crinkling of his jeans, and heavy breathing that matched her own. Anticipation built like a rising storm.

She wanted this man.

Jake stood in front of her, his cock sheathed. The back of his hand smoothed across her cheek before he cupped her face. His eyes sparked with a hunger she had never seen in a man.

"I've waited a lifetime to have you like this." He breathed the words before he captured her mouth.

Lifetime? She had only a moment of rational thought, before the kiss turned fiery. There was no tenderness, only a savage need in his touch, as his tongue plunged between her lips. Exploring and tasting every inch of her mouth, he flicked his tongue against hers. She responded in kind. He speared his fingers through her hair, holding her still as he took what he needed, drinking from her like a thirsty man.

It was maddening not to be able to touch him, to wrap her arms around him. Her hands grasped desperately at thin air, while her fingers tightened into fists. She yanked against her restraints, pushing her body close to his, her tongue piercing his mouth to taste him. Coffee, something sweet, and pure unadulterated maleness touched her taste buds.

She moaned deep into his mouth.

His fingers curled in her hair and sweet pain radiated to the roots, driving her mad with desire. But it was the ache in his voice as he spoke that made her blood run hot.

"God, I love the little noises you make." His nostrils flared as he scented her.

She felt the tremor that assailed him, as he released his hold to cup her face and kiss her once again. Strong, but gentle hands smoothed across her cheeks, caressing her neck, down her body, until he held her ass in his palms. He thrust his hips, parting her swollen folds.

Allie cried out at the incredible feeling, as her body welcomed him, closing around him like a gloved hand to pull him deeper. Slick and wet, he slid in easily to fill her completely.

Strong fingers dug into her ass. Each time he drew back, nearly pulling out of her pussy, she mourned the loss. But when he returned, pushed forward, driving deeper inside her, he rocked her body to her very soul. Over and over he thrust, ravishing her to the point she felt like she would explode.

She stared into the depths of his eyes. How could she not have seen the man hidden beneath the boy?

A butt-plug in her ass and Jake buried within her pussy was mind-blowing. He was muscle and strength, pure masculinity from his head to his toes.

Allie had never felt so aroused. She didn't know how much longer she could hold on. She trembled, perched on the edge of an orgasm so powerful her head spun.

"Breathe, honey," he urged. "Don't come until I say."

Her mouth opened and she gulped down a mouthful of much-needed air. How was she supposed to stop her impending climax? He was asking the impossible.

Jake must have realized how close she was because his pace slowed, easing in and out, tempting the flames of her desire. Her body gripped him tightly, frantically, trying to hold on to him.

It was hell—it was heaven.

Each penetrating thrust drove him against the back of her sex, setting off tremors that burst inside her. She leaned into him, seeking his warmth, wanting much more than she received.

Breathlessly Allie cried, "I need to touch you." The firestorm inside her made it impossible to remain silent. She was dying to caress him, needing something to hold onto as a rising tide of desire threatened to drown her. It built like a raging river beating at the floodgates.

But it was already too late. Her body jerked, a sudden contraction clenched and released, another followed, and another. "Oh God, Jake."

A wave of heat suffused her. It tore through her without mercy, making her cry out, the sound hoarse and strangled. She clawed the air with her fingers clenching and flexing, as one contraction after another twisted and raced throughout her body. Suddenly, her vision went dark. Was it because she squeezed her eyes shut or lack of oxygen from the intensity?

Weak and dizzy, trying to hold onto consciousness, she heard Jake's deep groan, felt his last thrust before he wrapped his arms around her and climaxed. Buried deep inside her his cock thickened, jerked violently several times, and then stilled.

Every muscle in his body melted against her. For a moment, he simply held her.

Releasing another soft moan, he eased away from her and disappeared into the master bathroom. Loud, running water told her that he'd turned on the bath water.

Allie hung listlessly from her bindings. Her knees felt like rubber, only her arms extended above her head kept her upright. Fur wrapped the handcuffs, but they bit into her wrists. She was too sated—too engulfed in what just happened to care.

Returning, the first thing he did was dislodge the butt-plug. Immediately she felt the loss, an emptiness that surprised her. So overwhelmed with the sensation, she had no idea what he did with the plug. The next thing she knew her ankles were free of their bindings. With the click of the handcuffs, her arms fell and she collapsed. If Jake hadn't been there to catch her, she would have fallen. He picked her up, cradling her like a baby against his chest. He rubbed his stubbled cheek against hers as he headed for the bathroom.

The water was warm and welcoming as he eased the both of them into the depths of the bathtub. A deep sigh of pleasure pushed from between her lips.

Back pressed to his chest, she relaxed against him. "Mmm...this feels so good."

With gentle fingertips, he brushed her hair aside and kissed her neck. "*You* feel so good." He wrapped his arms around her tightly.

She glanced over her shoulder. "I thought you were a shower kind of guy? You always use the hall bath."

He grinned. "A bath was the only way I could continue to hold you."

Silence lingered, nothing more said as they enjoyed the peaceful moment. Then he picked up a bar of soap and began to wash her body. Instantly, her nipples tightened, especially when he drew circles around them, plucking at them gently.

Allie turned in his arms, situating her knees on each side of his legs. Leaning forward, she slid her chest up and down his, now slick with soap.

"I missed you, Allie." His tender admission startled her, as had what he'd said earlier about waiting a lifetime. After she had graduated high school, she had been oblivious to everything around her, eager to begin an adventure and see the world.

Jake brushed back her hair, sliding his hand behind her head to pull her to his lips. He kissed her with so much passion, his mouth moving lightly and then hungrily across hers.

Allie would have never guessed that she had meant so much Jake. He had never given her any sign.

Now her life was a mess, they were at odds with each other over the house, but she wanted this moment with Jake. Wanted to believe that she hadn't lost everything that meant so much to her.

"Take me again, Jake." She captured his mouth in a fiery act of need.

Chapter Nine

Sex with Allie was incredible—better than Jake had imagined. Having her ask for more was beyond his wildest dreams. He still couldn't believe she was pressed tightly against him as they lounged naked in a bathtub of warm water. The scent of their lovemaking mingled with the soap he used to cleanse her body.

He cupped her face between his palms, brushed his lips across hers, kissing her as he spoke. "Anything you want, honey." There was nothing he wanted more than to lie with her again—to feel her warm, wet body surround and welcome his.

Without speaking, she rose, extending her hand to him. Desire heated her eyes, as she assisted him to his feet. Together they stepped out of the bathtub onto the mat. From one of the towel racks, she grabbed a big, fluffy towel and began to dry him. Carefully, she dried every inch of him. Her gentle caress across his cock and balls had him hardening in her hands.

Allie glanced up at him through heavy eyelids, an expression of pleasure upon her mouth—kiss-swollen lips that captured his attention. Just the thought of fucking her mouth made him hard. He couldn't wait to feel her lips around his cock. His fingers circled his erection and he began to pump slowly. She swallowed hard, the action sending his balls tight against his body.

"Come here." He extracted a dry towel from the rack. She stood quietly as he wiped the moisture from her naked body. As he set the cloth down, he said, "On your knees."

Her head jerked up to meet his gaze. Her brows pulled together, as if she thought of refusing him. But she wouldn't. He could see it in her lustful eyes. She wanted to taste him.

Freeing one hand, he grasped the back of her neck, pulling her close so that he could run his tongue along her lips. "Fuck me with that pretty mouth." Releasing her, he folded the towel and placed it on the cold wood flooring.

As she began to kneel, she used her hands against his hips to steady herself. Her breasts were the prettiest sight he had ever seen, so full and heavy, her nipples rosy and hard.

Halfway down, Jake stopped Allie. Tugging, he pulled her back into a standing position. "You have the sexiest titties." Leaning forward, he suckled one nipple and then the other, before he blew lightly on each of them. The skin around the shaded areola reacted, forming small bumps he traced with his finger. "Now on your knees."

After Allie obeyed, she reached for him. He dodged her grasp. "Place your hands behind your back." Again, he took himself in hand. His fingers tightened, as he slid them up and down his cock. A pearl of pre-come squeezed from the small slit. He ran his thumb over it, working the slick fluid over the head.

She glanced up at him with need in her gaze. "I want to touch you."

Jake shook his head. "I want to take you like this." Truth was he wouldn't last long if she stroked him. He stepped forward. "Place your hands behind your back." Cock in hand, he traced his erection over her lips.

She hesitated briefly, before complying. The movement thrust her breasts forward, inviting him to savor.

Jake couldn't help himself. He fell to his knees, releasing his cock so that both of his hands cupped her breasts. He fondled the heavy globes, as he pressed his lips to hers. When her arms snaked around his neck, he broke the kiss. "Keep your hands behind your back." He pinched her nipples hard. She gasped, her eyes darkening, before she dropped her arms to her sides. Teasingly, he laved each of her nipples with his tongue, before capturing one and then the other in his mouth to suckle. She arched into his touch, releasing a soft whimper.

She tasted so good. Felt even better in his hands, as he held her breasts and gently kneaded. He kissed her softly once more, before he released her and stood.

It made him hot to see her kneeling in a submissive manner, hands behind her back, waiting to take his cock deep within her mouth. He guided his erection toward her now-reddened lips. Close enough to touch, her lips parted, opening wide to receive him.

As her lips closed around his shaft, a tremor shook him. His breath caught. Blood rushed his balls. His erection hardened and lengthened more. Trembling fingers slipped through her silky, long hair to hold her firmly as his hips thrust forward.

Fuck! Was he dreaming?

He threw back his head, jaw clenched, as her warmth moved up and down his shaft. "Yeah." The single word came out half-strangled. The feel of her tongue stroking up one side and down the other was beyond anything he imagined. Yet when she sucked him to the back of her throat, her inner muscles clamping down on him, he nearly lost it. He tightened his grip in her hair.

"God," he groaned, low and long. His hips thrust in time with each stroke. She swallowed, her throat muscles squeezed him and his knees buckled. He caught himself by placing his hands on her shoulders.

Red-hot fire filled his balls. "Honey, I'm about to explode." He wanted to give her the opportunity to stop if she was uncomfortable with taking all of him.

A sense of pride filled him when she didn't break her stride. If anything, the vacuum-hold she held him with increased, driving him completely out of his mind.

"Allie—" Her name tore from his mouth as liquid heat burned down his cock.

She gagged slightly as his seed filled her mouth, but she didn't pull away, instead she swallowed over and over again, wringing out every bit of sensation from him. The intimacy of the act was so moving that his toes curled and a shiver raced up his back.

He was attempting to catch his breath when she released him and looked up. Lust simmered in the depths of her eyes. Her tongue made a sexy trail across her swollen lips.

"Allie," he moaned, again, reaching to help her to her feet. She came willingly to his arms. Chin resting on her head, he said, "Now it's my turn to taste you."

He wasn't finished with this woman. Just the thought of licking the cream between her thighs made him growl. The low, coarse sound brought her head up. She smiled softly at him.

Her arms snaked around his neck, before she pulled him close, pressing her lips to his. He could taste himself on her tongue, as he slanted his head and deepened the caress. Slowly he backed her out of the bathroom and into the bedroom. Scooping his arm beneath the back of her knees, he raised her into his arms. Without breaking the kiss, he walked to the bed.

Jake's heart pounded. The morning was unfolding into an unbelievable day. Allie was finally his.

Jake released her to stand. Then he went to the closet and found the new dark-brown, velour comforter he had bought along with the bed. Returning, he shook the spread out over the mattress. Without a word, she crawled upon the bed. She was so sexy; her pale body a contrast against the comforter. "You're so beautiful." He crawled in beside her. His larger body covered her smaller one. Immediately, her taut nipples hardened as they slid across the hair of his chest.

His lips caressed hers briefly, and then trailed a path down her neck, nipping and sucking, playing tentatively at each breasts. He flattened his tongue against each turgid peak, teasing them with slow circles into firmer nubs before moving further down her body. When he reached the patch of wheaten curls at the apex of her thighs, he inhaled her female musk.

"You smell good enough to eat." He savored the moment.

Light amusement bubbled from Allie's throat, as she fisted his hair. She spread her legs wider and drew him to the V of her thighs. "*Bon appétit.*"

Ready, she leaned back and closed her eyes.

Allie's clit throbbed, ached, waiting for Jake's touch. Her entire body tingled from pleasuring Jake. His essence lingered on her tongue. The scent of sex filled her nose.

He ran a single finger over the soft folds of her pussy. She moaned, needing more.

"You're so wet." His warm breath blew across her sensitive skin making her arch with need. She jerked when his tongue swiped her swollen folds. He caught her hips and held her steady. With long, wet strokes, he licked a path from one end of her slit to the other, flicking his tongue across her clit each time. She squirmed beneath his assault.

"Jake—" Her voice was breathless.

"What, honey?" he growled against her sex.

"I need you now."

Laughter met her request. Jake slipped a finger inside her, then two. "You're so tight and hot." He pulled her clit into his mouth and sucked hard, as he finger-fucked her, slow and steadily.

She whimpered, hips thrusting to the rhythm of his fingers pressing in and out of her body. As he replaced his fingers with his tongue, pushing deep within to taste her, she released a breathy groan of pleasure. The pinch in her belly tightened as the first signs of her oncoming climax appeared.

Heat rushed across her skin as a gush of wetness released between her legs. A rumble surfaced from somewhere deep in his chest, the husky vibration spreading through her chamber.

The wet sounds of him sucking sent tremors up her spine. Her entire body tensed. Exploded.

Rays of sensation ripped through her like a tornado, leaving no place untouched. It was incredible.

Jake pulled away. Her body still hummed with her release, as he moved across her to capture her lips. His kiss was hungry, wild. Tongues dueling, he pushed her legs unbelievably wider and entered her. He was thick and hard. The muscles beneath her palms flexed as she held on to his biceps. His heavy breathing signaled his oncoming orgasm.

She went rigid in his arms, breaking the caress of their mouths. "Condom. Stop, Jake. No condom." They had already tempted fate. She couldn't allow this to happen.

He froze, then went boneless, pressing her body into the mattress with his weight.

"I'm sorry." She felt the quiver that shook him with his apology. He did a push-up against the bed, rising to hover above her. "I'll be right back." The bed moaned, the bedsprings crying out, as he moved off the bed and stood.

Allie rose into a sitting position and watched his firm ass as he crossed the room. God, he was an Adonis from his rock-hard abs to his broad chest. Everything about him made her blood heat.

Using his mouth, he ripped open the condom package he had found in one of the boxes. Strong hands slid the protective sheath over his impressive erection. He glanced up, catching her gaze. His sinful smile made her melt inside like a marshmallow in rich hot chocolate.

Who would have ever guessed she'd be lying in bed with Jake O'Malley? Or that the boy next door would turn out to be the best lover she'd ever had? No one had ever made her feel so sexy, so fulfilled as Jake had.

He approached. Each step closer made her pulse quicken. She lay back down, sliding her legs apart, ready and willing to welcome him into her body once more.

Muscles rippled beneath his tanned skin, giving him almost a predatory air as he crawled on the bed. Heavy-lidded, he situated himself between her thighs. He smelled of sex and a special male scent that was his alone. His eyes were dark pools of desire. Warm to the touch, his hands caressed her legs, before he covered her body with his.

A single thrust of his hips, he parted her folds. Once again, he led her to the gates of heaven, filling her completely.

Yet, this time there was something different about the way he moved—almost cherishingly.

He fucked her slow, easing in and out of her body. His fingertips were light and gentle sliding across her cheek, touching her as if she was a gift to treasure. His sultry, penetrating expression made her feel that he had no eyes for another woman.

He desired her—only her.

It was silly, but the need to believe he wanted her burned behind her eyes, even as chills raced across her skin, beading her nipples into hard peaks. Their bodies rocked together, the bedsprings moaning beneath their weight. When he reached between them to caress her clit, something broke inside her. She threw back her head, arched her back and groaned soft and low with her release. Allie had felt nothing like this before. Her orgasm was poignant, piercing her heart—her soul.

One last thrust and Jake pressed deep into her cradle and moaned. His utterance was just as heartfelt before he collapsed atop her.

In the aftermath, Allie wrapped her arms around him, listening to his heavy breathing, loving the tenderness of the moment. All too soon, he rolled over to his side. His fingertips brushed the hair out of her eyes, before he leaned forward and pressed his lips to hers.

"It's good to have you home, Allie." He smiled, nuzzled her nose with his, and then rolled onto his back.

Home?

Time was ticking. She glanced at the clock sitting on the nightstand. Only an hour remained before she met with her mother's attorney about the ownership of the house. She didn't want to dampen the moment, but if they could settle this between them maybe it wouldn't become messy. Maybe they could have the time to see where their relationship might lead.

Allie rose up on an elbow. "Jake. We need to talk."

As if she had lit a flame beneath him, he popped out of bed and crossed the room. He bent to retrieve his jeans.

"Jake, please. We have to resolve this issue with the house."

She could almost hear his neck crackle as he snapped his head around while he jerked on his pants. "No."

She sat up straighter. "Ignoring the problem and thinking it'll go away won't work." He had put her off long enough. They had to settle this.

Her hormones had let this situation between her and Jake get out of control. It only made what she had to do more difficult.

The tendons in his neck bulged. "Allie, I own this house. Nothing's going to change that." He squared his shoulders. He was an impenetrable force as he approached her. "I want you to stay here." He paused for a moment before continuing, "And there's that issue of the other night." His voice softened as he referred to their first sexual exploration without a condom.

"Sell the house back to me."

"I can't. I have everything I own tied up in this house." She saw the truth in his sad expression.

Dammit. This was a mess.

Big tears filled her eyes, making her vision blurry. She glanced around the room. Everything of her mother's was gone, except for a picture of her on Jake's nightstand. In fact, it was a picture of all three of them in Sedona.

Overwhelmed by the truth that stared her in the face, she rose and quickly started gathering her clothes.

"Allie?" He reached for her, but she dodged his grasp. Clutching her clothes tightly to her chest, she pivoted, yanked the door open, and ran down the hallway.

Chapter Ten

Although Allie and Jake had shared an amazing morning, she couldn't let that deter her from what she needed to do. There probably wasn't a dead man's chance in hell to get her house back, but she had to try. Maybe there was a legal loophole. The house was all she had of her mother. The thought left her on the verge of tears as she pushed open the door to Mr. Allen's office.

The aged man, as much of a historical figure as the old museum on the intersection of Gilbert and Elliot roads, stood next to the water cooler. His even older secretary was nowhere in sight. A knobby finger raised his wire-rimmed glasses. He gave Allie a speculative once over, snubbing his nose at her jeans with reproach.

Always the picture of professionalism, his dark gray suit was immaculate compared to the blue T-shirt she had yanked out of her suitcase. She tried to smooth out the wrinkles, but it was no use.

The man she remembered hadn't changed much. Well, maybe he was older, grayer—no, make that balder. She could have sworn he was half a head shorter too.

"Well, missy, you've grown up." His voice was scratchy. He sipped once, twice from the cup he held, before he continued. "So what's this I hear that you aren't happy with how I handled your mother's affairs?" In less than a second, he had set the tone of the meeting.

Defensive.

Allie followed suit. "Happy?" she huffed with sarcasm in her voice. "You sold my house."

"Debts." He leaned toward the water cooler, re-filled his cup, and set it down on the desk. "Debts first—inheritance later."

Acid swirled in her stomach. She tried to calm herself by inhaling and releasing a breath slowly.

"Two mortgages and a slew of doctor's bills." Mr. Allen yanked off his glasses, pulled a handkerchief from his pocket and wiped the lenses, before settling them once again on his nose. "I tried to contact you. Mabel even hired a private investigator." He shook his head with an expression that looked close to disgust. "Foreclosure proceedings on the house began a month before your mother passed."

Tears beat at the back of Allie's eyelids.

She bit her bottom lip and prayed for strength. It had never been her style to beat around the bush. She came here for one reason and one reason only. "What can I do to get my house back?"

Once again, the old fart gave her a condemning glare, staring down his nose. "Ask young O'Malley to sell."

Please. Please. Please. Don't let this be my only choice.

The muscles in her throat tightened. "He won't."

Mr. Allen's glasses slid down his nose again. He used the same finger to reposition them. "It looks like you're out of luck. He legally owns the house."

"There has to be something I can do?" She hated the desperation in her voice and the tear that fell before she could hold it back.

Mr. Allen shook his head, turned and disappeared into his office, dismissing her.

"Well, so much for asking him about the issue with Brayer." Allie wasn't one to give up, but she knew when she was beaten. The house was Jake's. She couldn't stand admitting the truth, but there was no other alternative.

Allie moved toward the door, pulled it open as the self-closing spring triggered, almost striking her in the ass as she stepped beyond it and outside. The pungent smell of a carob tree assailed her as another unwanted tear fell.

Her heavy footsteps carried her down the sidewalk. Birds chirping in the big ash tree she passed didn't faze her. The Walgreen's Pharmacy across the street did. She remembered the other reason why she came to town.

A pregnancy test.

Commercials on television announced the tests nowadays were so accurate pregnancy was detectable days after conception. With a little luck, she could at least put that issue to rest.

A tremor shook her. What if she was pregnant?

"No." Allie squared her shoulders. Being pregnant was out of the question. She waited for the traffic to thin and then darted across the street.

The heavy glass door screeched as she pushed it open and went inside the drugstore. A cool breeze greeted her along with an array of perfume scents. Her nose twitched with the different fragrances. She gave her nose a rub, before heading toward the back of the store where the large pharmacy sign hung.

Her eyes widened when she looked at the shelves of products. "Oh my God. There are so many." Yet one in particular drew her eye—EPT, Early Pregnancy Test. She grabbed the package off the shelf and headed for the front of the store, picking up a bottle of Tylenol for the budding headache that needled the back of her eyelids. She thought of her prescription medication, but Allie needed her wits about her.

The girl behind the counter smiled. "Will this be all?"

"Yes." Allie pushed her hand into her pocket and extracted a twenty.

Change and bag in hand, she left the store. She had driven her mother's old Grand Am to town, a car that now belonged to Jake as well. He had let her borrow it.

Borrow. My own mother's car.

How did her life get so screwed up?

She stepped off the curb to cross the street and jerked to a stop as a kid on a bicycle passed within a hair of her. Her heart stuttered. The breath she held came out in a rush. "Crap! That was close."

Trying to pull herself together, she crossed the street and headed for her mother's car. The car door moaned in protest as she opened it, slid inside, tossing the bag and spilling its contents on the seat next to her. For a moment, she sat numb to all that had happened just staring at the pregnancy test. Time passed and then she raised her hips and reached inside her pocket to retrieve the keys. It took several attempts to insert the key because she was shaking so badly. Finally, she switched the car on and the engine roared to life.

She shifted the car into drive, released her foot from the brake and eased into traffic. Allie had no idea where she was heading until she saw the cemetery in the distance. As if on autopilot, she steered the vehicle beneath the wrought iron gates.

It was time to face what she had rejected since she came back to town. Time to face reality.

Acres and acres of neatly manicured land lay before her. Every couple of feet artificial or real flowers sprung from the ground, marking a grave. Only then did Allie realize that she had no idea if she was in the correct cemetery or where her mother was buried.

The sudden heaviness in her chest was too much. Tears welled in her eyes as she pulled the car over to the side. She barely managed to switch the engine off before the wall holding back her emotions burst. A scream tore from her throat, releasing the pent-up fury and pain inside.

"*Momma.*" The single word came out a desperate cry. "I'm so sorry, Momma." Allie wrapped her arms around her chest and rocked back and forth, trying to chase the guilt and regret away, but nothing helped.

The pain in her heart didn't ease up and neither did her tears.

Only when her chest squeezed and she felt dizzy did she attempt to pace her breathing. Forehead pressed to the steering wheel, she sniffled, trying to grasp some semblance of control.

Allie was alone in this world. Her mother was gone. Brayer Tech thought her responsible for the sabotage in Peru.

Jake was the only person on earth who she felt close to—trusted. Not even thoughts of Tom consoled her like they did when she thought of Jake. Allie had never felt anything as explosive or genuine as she did with Jake. Problem was he now owned what she wanted—her home. As if her thoughts conjured him, he stood outside her car tapping gently on the window.

She swiped at her tears, before she rolled the window down. "What are you doing here?"

Concern brightened his eyes. "I was passing by and saw your car." His voice softened. "You all right, Allie?"

She wanted to scream at him, "*Do I look all right?*" but she held her tongue. Instead, she nodded, forcing back the need to strike out at someone—anyone—especially Jake.

"Honey, you're on the wrong side of the cemetery."

Allie swallowed hard, fighting back her emotions. "I don't know where she is." Her voice sounded weak, almost childlike, even to her.

"I know." He opened the door and stepped away so she could get out. "Walk with me. I'll show you."

A light breeze stirred her blonde hair, brushing it across her shoulders and into her face. She tucked the strands behind her ear. As her arm came back to her side, Jake scooped her hand in his. Warm and strong, his fingers felt good around hers.

Together, they walked on the asphalt and followed the winding road. When they came to where a large pine tree stood, he took her off the path and led her to a grave with a fresh bouquet of white roses, her mother's favorite flowers.

Allie glanced at Jake. "Your flowers?"

He nodded.

She pulled from his grasp and fell to her knees. Her hand shook as she traced her mother's name on the gray marble stone, with the words *Precious mother and friend* engraved beneath her name.

Allie was speechless, but she did manage to ask, "You?"

Again, Jake nodded.

Unshed tears choked her, as she gazed up at him. "Why?"

The muscles in his neck bulged. She watched his jaw clench, before he opened his mouth. "Mabel was my friend. She—she was like a mother to me when my own passed away."

The truth shone in his bright eyes. He had cared deeply for Allie's mother. He, too, mourned her passing.

Allie pushed to her feet and leaned into Jake, wrapping her arms around his waist and held on tightly. He pressed his chin to the top of her head and sighed aloud.

Fighting back emotion, her chin trembled. "I miss her, Jake."

He combed his fingers through her hair. "I know, honey. I miss her too."

"What am I going to do?"

She was unaware she had spoken aloud, until he said, "There's nothing more to do. I've taken care of everything."

It was true. He had been there for her mother when she hadn't. A fresh wave of guilt rose, pulling her from his arms. She started walking back to her car.

The boots he wore padded softly against the grass as he followed her. "Allie?"

"I need to be alone, Jake." Too many things had happened. She didn't even know where she belonged any more. Everything was slipping from her grasp. Misty-eyed, she whirled on the soles of her shoes to face him once again. "The house is all I have left of her." Her voice was tight and shaky. "Now it's gone too."

Jake's features hardened. He ran his fingers through his wavy, black hair. "Dammit, Allie. I can't sell it to you." Exasperation filled his voice. His shoulder barely touched hers as he breezed by and headed for his truck.

Crap. Allie didn't know what to do. Even if Jake had agreed to sell her the house, after making the down payment, she probably couldn't get credit, not without a job. That particular problem hadn't occurred to her until now.

If only she could remember what happened that night, she might be able to get her life back into order.

Jake's wrapped his fingers tightened around the steering wheel. He understood Allie's dilemma, but what was he suppose to do? He hadn't expected her to return home, especially after her long absence. Falling into bed with her had only complicated matters. Now that he had tasted her, he was reluctant to give her up. Still, he knew that when Allie's feet got restless she'd be gone in a heartbeat. His gut twisted with the thought.

As he guided his truck into a parking spot at Fry's Market, he thought of Mabel. Would she approve of him and Allie in a relationship? Her approval meant everything to him.

The vehicle's door moaned as he opened it and climbed out. "Have to remember to pick up some WD-40." The grind of the door when he opened it was due to a recent romp in the desert. Dust created havoc in all working mechanics.

A hefty yank, he dislodged a shopping cart from the long line of them. Two teenage girls around sixteen giggled, whispering behind their hands as he passed them. He couldn't help the smile that surfaced when he heard one say, "Hot."

The strong scent of flowers hit him as he stepped through the sliding glass doors. His refrigerator was empty, with the exception of a couple of beers. Steaks barbequing on the grill sounded inviting, as did a loaded baked potato. He maneuvered his cart toward the vegetable aisle.

"Jake."

He turned when he heard his name. A flashy redhead grinned at him. Leslie had been his most recent lover, but she had left on a job assignment in San Diego. The rich tan she wore said she had enjoyed the California sun.

Her womanly scent enveloped him as she gave him a kiss on the cheek followed by her soft confession. "I've missed you." A yellow ribbon held her long hair in a ponytail, but a few tendrils framed her face and tickled his neck.

"Missed you too." He took a step backward when he saw a mother and her son come around the corner. "When did you get back?"

Leslie tugged a loose thread from the frilled edges of her shirt. "Yesterday." She pushed down the sleeves of her yellow sweater that hung slightly off her shoulders, giving that sexy, come-and-get-me look. "Did you buy the Grant house? Move in yet?"

"Yeah. I've got this weekend to move all my stuff out of my old place." He grabbed the handle of his cart and headed toward the display piled high with brown and red potatoes.

As he picked up a five-pound bag and placed it into his cart, she said "Cooking tonight?" One of her brows rose.

He knew she was fishing for an invitation, but he wasn't going there. "Yes." With a little luck, he and Allie would repeat this morning's activity. She had been so willing—so sexy. His cock stirred with the memory of how her body responded to his. Her sweet cries of surrender still rang in his ears.

Leslie's copper gaze stroked him with interest, paying special attention to his now bulging crotch. He pivoted, pushing his cart toward a display of asparagus.

Standing beside him, she picked up an ear of corn. Stared him straight in the eyes, as her fingers closed around the vegetable and she slid her hand up and down it seductively.

"Someone I know?" Through feathered eyelashes, she looked up at him. Her tongue made a sexy path along her bottom lip.

Well, shit. His cock hardened even more as he reached for a bundle of the green vegetables and placed it in his cart. Now this was awkward. There wasn't any way to face the question, except head-on. "Alison. She's back."

As Leslie's eyes widened, shock flitted across her face. "What? Did she come with the house?" Leslie was quick with the sassy comment.

"Yes— I mean no." An uneasy huff burst from his mouth. "It's a long story."

"I bet it is." He heard the bite in Leslie's voice.

She was jealous.

What they had was sexual. Clearly, he was the only one who felt that way. Not once had they talked about a relationship. *Hell*, he never could get Allie out of his head, much less promise himself to another.

He firmed his tone. "Leslie, her mother just passed away and she has nowhere to go."

"Nowhere to go?" She released a quick, weighty breath of disbelief. "So she's taken up residence in her old room or your new one?"

He pushed his cart out of the produce section, wondering if he moved fast enough whether he could lose her around the aisle of alcohol they were entering. "I'm not having this conversation with you." He scanned the bottles of wine to his left and right, choosing a Merlot before he moved on.

"Wine?" Her tone rose in pitch.

He yanked his cart to a stop. "Leslie…" Her name came out as a reprimand.

"*Fine.*" She glanced at her wristwatch. "I've got to go."

He was never so relieved as when she turned her back to him and walked away.

Leslie had been a fun and willing partner, but she never could fill his need for Allie. Nevertheless, there was no telling when Allie would be gone. But he would do his utmost to keep her as long as she'd stay.

Maybe longer, he thought, remembering the pregnancy test he saw on the seat of the car next to her when he tapped on her window at the cemetery.

Chapter Eleven

The telephone screeched as Allie descended the stairs. She raised her chin, inhaling deeply. Something smelled good. The growl churning her stomach reminded her that she hadn't eaten all day. Already her jeans were looser.

Another peal of the telephone and she hastened her steps.

She reached for the telephone at the bottom of the stairs and pulled her hand back. This wasn't her house. The call couldn't be for her.

"Get that, will you?" Jake yelled. He sounded too far away to be in the kitchen—backyard?

Oh, yeah. That's where that delicious aroma was coming from.

Allie raised the receiver to her ear. "Hello."

No response, but she could hear heavy breathing.

"Hello," she repeated. A click sounded and then a dial tone.

As she placed the receiver in the cradle, Jake poked his head around the kitchen door. "Who was it?"

Damn, you're good-looking.

Only in Arizona could people wear shorts in the dead of winter. She eyed his brawny calves, moving her gaze over thick thighs, before taking in his narrow hips clad in shorts and the skin-tight T-shirt that molded his chest. She hated to admit it, but the man before her was the best lay she had ever had. Not to mention turning out to be the best friend she had ever had.

"Heavy breather." She cleared her throat, trying to ease the burn that began to simmer in her belly.

His smile faded in place of a sorrowful expression. "My first and I missed it."

"Maybe he'll call back."

"Funny." He threw the potholder he held at her. "Come help me with the salad."

She caught the potholder as she moved toward the kitchen. "I'm invited to stay for dinner?"

He was already out the arcadia doors to address the building smoke that began to billow from the barbeque outside. The smoky scent of mesquite filled the air blowing into the kitchen.

Her stomach growled again as she looked around her mother's kitchen. Gone was the warm, inviting aroma of cookies or bread baking in the oven. Her mother had loved to bake.

The kitchen looked much like when Allie left. The California fruit labels her mother had framed hung from the walls. Herbs lined the kitchen window, copper pots hung from above the stove. The arcadia doors were open on summer evenings when the day cooled off. Her mother loved the fresh air.

Night had fallen. Stars glistened above, as a whisper of clouds streaked the sky. It didn't matter where she was in the world, the heavens were still beautiful.

"Hey, a little help here." She startled at Jake's voice. His brows tugged down, as he approached. "You okay?" His warm hand slid up her bare arm. In lieu of moving away, she leaned into him wanting the comfort he offered—knowing it was wrong, but needing it anyway.

Truthfully, she was afraid the last words they had spoken would set the tone for tonight.

His lips were soft against hers, as he pulled her into his arms. "You okay, honey?" he whispered against her ear.

How was she supposed to answer? The man who held her so tenderly was the same one who stood between her and the home she'd been raised in.

"Yeah. Just a little weary." Her stomach groaned. "And hungry."

His face lit up with a smile. He released her and moved quickly toward the sliding glass doors. "Medium?"

"What?" she asked, coming to lean against the doorframe.

His broad back faced her, giving her a perfect view of his firm ass. "Your steak. You like it medium?"

Amazed, she nodded even though he couldn't see her. "How did you remember?"

He looked over his shoulder. "I remember a lot about you, Allie." The intensity in his gaze and the certainty in his tone sent a shiver up her spine. The heat in his eyes made her body burn. Her nipples firmed and the spot between her thighs dampened.

Why had she been so blind about Jake all those years ago? Maybe it was her immaturity. Maybe she had been too absorbed in herself and wanting to see the world. Whatever it was, she had to admit she'd missed a lot overlooking him. She dragged her gaze over his masculine physique. Remembered how his touch—his kiss—turned her on.

Or was he the only way she could hold onto her home? She released a sigh and turned around to start the salad.

Into two small salad bowls, she hand-pinched the large leaves of lettuce into pieces. Four years ago, before she'd left home, he'd asked to go with her. She tossed a handful of cherry tomatoes and sliced cucumbers upon the lettuce. Like always, she had brushed him off. She still remembered his hurt expression as he had turned and walked away. As she sprinkled grated cheese over the salad, something told her she had been a fool that day.

Jake had grown to be a wonderful, caring man. And he was fucking hot between the sheets.

Carrying the bowls to the table, she glanced out the door at him as he forked the steaks and placed them on a large platter. Memories of their morning, bound before him as he took what he wanted, made her breathing elevate. She couldn't help wondering what he would look like spread eagle before her. What it would feel like to do anything she desired with him at her mercy. With more effort than she cared to admit, she pushed the thought from her head and headed for the cupboard to set the table.

A bottle of red wine sat on the counter. Allie fished through the drawer, found her mother's old corkscrew and began to peel off the foil around the bottle top.

"Let me do that." Jake's warm hands slid over hers, relieving her of the chore. "Your mother always had a hell of a time with this old thing. Mine is packed away."

Allie wrung her hands together. "Jake, did she suffer?"

His hands stilled and he looked at her hard. "I don't think so, Allie. The worst was missing you and not knowing what happened. I won't lie, it nearly drove her insane wondering if you were alive."

Guilt surfaced like an imminent wave. Allie hadn't been the only one affected this past year.

"Those damn private investigators from Brayer Tech hounded her relentlessly." He began to open the wine. A firm yank made the cork release with a pop. "Not to mention tailed her."

What the fuck? Did Brayer think her mother was involved? Anger chased away the guilt she felt.

"Allie, Mabel never gave up on you." The red wine swished into a goblet as he tilted the bottle and poured. "Told me you'd be home some day and then everything would be okay."

Allie accepted the glass he handed her, bringing it to her lips.

"You know she read your letters over and over again. She was so proud of you."

The fruity scent touched her nose as she sipped the sweet, woodsy wine. It went down smoothly, but not his words.

Allie had put her mother through hell. Acid churned in her stomach. She felt sick. What the hell happened the night her campsite was attacked? Why couldn't she remember anything?

"Jake." She squeezed her eyes, fighting back feelings of regret that rushed up to engulf her.

One... She inhaled a deep breath. *Two...Three...*

Allie opened her eyes. Her hand trembled as her fingers tightened around the stem of the glass. "Thank you for being here for her."

He reached for her glass setting both hers and his upon the counter with a clink. Before Allie knew it, she was in his arms. Being held by this man was becoming a habit she could get used to as she basked in his strength.

"I would have done anything for Mabel." His chin rested on top of her head. "I loved her, Allie."

Like I love you. Jake barely held the words back, as he tightened his grip on the woman he held.

It was true.

He had loved Allie almost all his life. Some might have called it infatuation or obsession. She was never far from his mind, nor did he give up on the thought that some day they would be together.

He inhaled, trying to get a rein on his emotions. “Come on, let’s eat.” As he pulled out her chair and she sat, the doorbell rang. “Who could that be?” Visitors were not welcome at this moment.

The melodic beat rose and fell, again.

Grinning, she gazed up at him. “You won’t know until you answer it.”

He jerked around and walked out of the kitchen into the living room. He folded his fingers around the doorknob but before he opened the door, he leaned in and peered through the peephole. He knocked his forehead against the door, and an exasperated breath left his lungs.

Leslie.

The porch light bathed her in a spotlight, highlighting all her features, especially the skin-tight little black dress and stiletto heels she wore. Leslie was dressed for seduction.

“What are you doing here?” he mumbled to himself.

This wasn’t good—wasn’t good at all.

“Who is it?” came Allie’s voice from behind him.

“No one,” he threw over his shoulder, catching a glimpse of her as she waltzed into the living room. “Just go back into the kitchen.” His words forced one of her brows to arch. That stubborn look he had come to know flashed across her face.

The doorbell sang again.

Without making a move toward the kitchen, she asked, “Gonna answer the door?”

He pulled the door back. Leslie threw open her arms and yelled, "Surprise!"

No shit, he wanted to say. "Leslie, this isn't a good time."

Allie frowned.

Leslie gave Allie one of her famous smiles—no teeth, but there was a bite to it. "Allie!" Leslie released him, sauntered over to Allie, and pulled her into her arms. "You're back from the jungles." The women knew each other from school.

Trapped in Leslie's embrace, Allie's frown deepened, as she glared at Jake. "Leslie?" she mumbled like it was a question.

"Oh, my gosh." She released Allie. "You'll have to tell me all about it." Before Jake knew what was happening he was in Leslie's arms again. "Sugar, I missed you so much." She squeezed him as if she truly did miss him, but he knew it was for Allie's benefit and it appeared to be working.

Allie's eyes widened. Jake felt his skin shrivel beneath her glare. Not good—not good at all.

"Leslie." He lowered his voice in warning, extracting himself from Leslie's death grip. Talk about awkward. Both women pinned their gazes on him. One hopeful, the other filled with heat.

Leslie raised her nose and inhaled. "Mmmm...something smells good."

"We were just sitting down to eat." A smile softened Allie's face, but not her eyes. "Why don't you join us?"

Jake reached for the door. "Leslie was just leaving."

She gazed up at him sweetly. "My plans have been canceled. I'd love to stay."

Allie pivoted, but instead of walking toward the kitchen, she headed for the stairs. "Better yet, I wanted to take in a movie tonight." She shot a glance over a shoulder. "You two enjoy dinner and catch up." There was a sting to her last words that Jake didn't miss.

More than irritated, he pulled his arm out of Leslie's grip. Heat raced up his neck, stinging his ears. "That wasn't necessary." He didn't try to hide his anger.

Leslie straightened her backbone and lowered her eyelashes, looking up at him innocently. "I thought there was something between us."

"Leslie, I made no promises." He stared up the stairs. "Allie came home to her whole world turned upside down."

"Not my problem."

Jake jerked his attention back to the smug-looking woman beside him who spoke so coldly.

He was about to tell Leslie exactly what he thought of her when Allie bounded down the stairs. Her boots tapped hard against each step as she shoved her arms through a light jacket. Not a word spoken, she breezed by them.

"Allie, wait."

She ignored him, whipping open the door and pulling it shut behind her. At the thud, Jake turned to Leslie. "You might as well leave too."

Her copper eyes widened. "What? You're going after her?" She reached for him, but he moved out of her grasp.

"No. I'm not. But I don't feel like company either."

"Jake," she whined, "we can work this out."

He was about to show her the way out when he heard tires squeal. His first thought was that Allie was pissed.

The pop of gunfire told him it was much more.

Heart in his throat, he yanked the door wide, sending it banging against the wall. Adrenaline buzzed in his veins as he saw the taillights of a speeding car and Allie crumbled facedown upon the moist grass of his front yard. Heart pounding, he ran to her side, sliding to his knees.

"Allie." His hands trembled as he reached for her, stopping to linger above her shoulders, afraid to touch her—afraid not to. "Call an ambulance." Fear made his voice tremble. He glanced up to see Leslie frozen where she stood, an expression of horror twisting her pretty features.

"Now!" he yelled, shaking her into action. She fled toward the house.

Gently, he rolled Allie over. Anger and alarm coursed through his body like liquid fire as something warm and wet touched his hand.

Blood.

Lots of blood.

Allie's blood.

It streamed down her forehead, cheek, gushing onto her jacket. Moonlight threw shadows across her face as he sat, pulling her onto his lap.

Panic choked him. He had to stop the flow.

Pressing his hand against her head, her life essence continued to ooze between his fingers. His other hand trembled, as he felt for the pulse in her throat. For a moment, he couldn't find the beat.

"No." It was a plea. Relief spread throughout, when he felt the swish, weak and fragile, beneath his finger.

"Where is that damned ambulance?" he yelled, as his hand moved across her body looking for any other possible injuries. When he couldn't find another wound, he pulled her close and held her, rocking back and forth. "Wake up, honey, please wake up."

Cell phone in hand, Leslie flew out the front door as if she had wings. She was breathless. "They're coming." He heard tears in her tone. "Oh God, Jake, is she okay?"

A cool breeze ruffled his hair. "Shot at least once—in the head. I can't get her to wake up." If only she'd open her eyes, speak to him. A tremor shook him to his core. He needed to hear her voice.

Leslie cupped her palm over her mouth, before dragging the telephone to her ear. "She's been shot. No. She isn't conscious." She relayed a couple more things to the 9-1-1 operator, but Jake didn't hear her words above his silent ones praying Allie would be okay.

"What's taking them so long?" Jake growled, applying more pressure to the wound. The blood on his hands started to thicken and grow sticky. Fresh blood continued to seep between his fingers.

"Uh, huh. Yes." Leslie appeared calmer as she spoke with the operator. "When? They're coming, Jake."

In the distance the faint sound of sirens rose. The shrill grew louder as they neared, until finally he saw the strobe of red and blue lights.

A flood of police cruisers rushed from the north and south. Tires screeched. Voices rose as several officers scrambled from the cars. Their movements were cautious, as one officer began to issue commands. Uniformed officers blended in with the night as they swarmed the neighborhood, two of them heading toward Jake.

"Sir, release her. Get to your feet and move away," a female officer demanded with her hand resting on her gun. The male cop next to her had his hand poised and ready for any problems. "Now," she said firmly.

Mixed emotions rattled Jake as he scanned their hardened faces. He knew the police were just doing their job, but he felt paralyzed. “She’s hurt.” His voice sounded lost as he spoke to the woman whose badge reflected the name Collins.

“Yes, sir. We need to assess her condition. Move away. *Now.*” Impatience heated Collins’ tone, as she and her partner descended upon Jake. The male officer grabbed Jake’s arm at the same time Collins knelt, taking a hold of Allie to lay her gently on the ground. She didn’t move. Blood continued to flow from her head wound.

From her pocket, Collins extracted a pair of latex gloves and quickly put them on. “I need gauze and a blanket here.” She wasted no time locating Allie’s vitals and applying pressure against the wound. Another officer approached, handing the woman several pads of gauze, which she applied to Allie’s wound. Without hesitation, the man began to spread the blanket over Allie, tucking it tightly beneath her.

They were treating her for shock. Why hadn’t Jake thought of that?

He tried to shrug out of the officer’s grasp. But the man blocked him with his body, wedging himself between Allie and Jake. A fuzzy voice came over the officer’s radio. With an uncompromising stance, he shoved his hand out toward Jake. “Stay put.” At the same time, he leaned his head into the radio on his shoulder, pushed a button and answered. “Area clear. Proceed.”

The fire truck that had stopped down the street began to move toward them. In the distance, Jake saw Leslie speaking with another officer.

“Your name?”

Jake’s attention snapped to the officer before him.

"Jake O'Malley." Jake glanced at the officer's badge that revealed the man's name was Layton.

After the fire engine pulled up in front of the house and stopped, five firefighters jumped out of the truck. A redheaded man dressed in a jacket, navy blue shirt and pants came immediately to Jake's side. "What's her name?"

"Allie Grant. Alison," Jake corrected.

The fire captain, a dark-haired lanky man Jake heard referred to as Larry, started slinging orders. "Laurie, take C-spine. Gary, backboard, check pulse and respiration. I'll start the heart monitor."

As they worked on Allie, Officer Layton asked, "Are you her husband?" The redheaded firefighter stood close, listening.

Husband? Jake felt a scowl pull at his brows. "No, friend. I'm her friend." He swallowed hard, moving so he could see what they were doing to Allie.

"Are you okay?" the firefighter asked.

Jake yanked his head around to stare at the man. "Me? Yeah?" The man studied him, particularly the blood on Jake's hands.

"Can you tell me what happened?" Officer Layton asked, while several police in the distance began to cordon off the area. Radios squeaked and clicked. Neighbors had already begun to flood the street, cautioned back into their homes for safety.

"What happened?" Officer Layton repeated.

Jake shook his head. He should have never let Allie leave. The sight of her lying there, not moving, chilled him to the bone. "Shots. I heard shots."

And there was so much blood. It still oozed from her head. The sharp acrid scent was heavy in the cool air. A chill shook Jake.

He mumbled something about running out of the house, as the short blonde firefighter named Laurie moved swiftly but cautiously, securing a brace around Allie's neck and stabilizing her head. In one fluid motion, the captain rolled Allie to her side and Gary slid a backboard against her back. When she was lying flat, he secured the straps around her body and immediately began taking her vitals.

"What?" Jake jerked his gaze from Allie to Officer Layton.

"Did you see the gunman?" he repeated.

"No. Taillights. That's all. Fucking taillights." Jake brushed his bloody fingers through his hair. "Then Allie lying on the ground."

"Do you know if she's allergic to anything?" the firefighter asked.

"Allergic? No," Jake responded as if he was on autopilot.

"Taking any medications?"

"No—yeah. Something for headaches, I think."

"How many shots did you hear?" It was Officer Layton's turn to ask the questions.

"One. Two." Was it only one? Jake felt like he was losing it. "Fuck. I don't know."

The sound of material ripping yanked his gaze back to Allie.

Sharp trauma shears cut through her jeans like butter. One leg and then the other, Gary stripped her of her pants and shirt until she lay naked for all eyes to see.

Cold, Jake thought over modesty. "Can't they cover her up?" He tried to move closer to her, but both Officer Layton and the firefighter Jake named Red, intervened, wedging their bodies between him and Allie.

"Jake." Red used his name as if they were friends instead of complete strangers. "They need to check for additional wounds. Would you like to go into the house and sit down?"

"Hell, no," Jake barked.

The captain glanced quickly toward Laurie. "Start high flow O2, fifteen liters, non-rebreather."

The female firefighter tore open a sealed package, withdrew a mask with an inflatable bag. The disposed paper fell to the ground as she slipped the oxygen mask over Allie's nose and mouth.

Allie remained deathly still. A slight cloudiness against the mask told Jake she breathed.

The firefighters moved quickly and efficiently, raising the backboard to lift Allie into the air. Their footsteps were hasty as they headed toward the ambulance.

When did the ambulance get here? Jake's mind was numb. He took several quick steps toward her. "Is she going to be okay? Where are you taking her?"

"Good Samaritan. It's the closest Level One Trauma Unit," Officer Layton responded, never leaving his side, Red close behind them.

Allie's eyelashes fluttered, as the backboard touched the gurney outside the ambulance.

Jake's pulse leaped.

"*Where...am...I...*?" Allie slurred her words, each one came out unbelievably slow and muffled through the oxygen mask.

"Allie!" Jake pushed past Officer Layton and Red. Allie's eyelids were droopy. "Honey, are you okay?" He tried to grasp her hand, but the two firefighters pushed the gurney into the ambulance and climbed in beside her.

"*Where...am...I...?*" she repeated, just as lethargic as the first time. She sounded as if she was on a two-day drunk. Her head was immobilized. He knew she couldn't see anything but what was directly above her, the white headliner of the vehicle and bright lights. He thought he heard her voice shake, as she asked, "*W-w-who are you?*"

The captain ripped open a package containing tubing. "I'm Captain Jenson, Larry Jenson."

As the ambulance driver and paramedic climbed into the front of the ambulance, the captain and Laurie began to work on placing intravenous lines in both of Allie's arms.

"Lock and go," Captain Jenson yelled.

Gary slammed the door shut. With a jerk, the vehicle lurched forward, sirens blaring and lights flashing.

Jake's heart leaped into his throat. "Is she going to be okay? She didn't act like she knew where she was."

"That's normal for head trauma victims. She'll be in a daze, repeat her words." Red placed his hand on Jake's shoulder. "Would you like to ride to the hospital with us?"

"No. I'll follow in my truck."

The man squeezed Jake's shoulder. "Be careful, buddy." Then he turned and headed for the fire engine.

"Mr. O'Malley, I have more questions, but you can answer them at the hospital," Office Layton informed him.

Without waiting for permission to leave, Jake ran for his truck.

Chapter Twelve

God-awful pain splintered throughout Allie's skull, forcing her eyes shut. The sensation of her head ripping in two made her moan. Even moaning hurt.

"Don't move. Two more minutes." The X-ray technician's voice sounded tinny coming from somewhere in the tube Allie found herself lying in.

Don't move? She was naked, except for a thin sheet draped over her, strapped to a backboard, and her head immobilized. All she could see was directly above her.

And the tech had the nerve to say don't move.

A wave of nausea swooped over Allie. She groaned again. Eyes squeezed tightly, she tried to focus on the steady ticking of the MRI and not the bitter bile crawling up her throat.

Relief was a welcome sensation when she felt the motion of the machine, but when she raised her eyelids, the bright lights of the room were like daggers piercing her eyes.

"I know it hurts, dear, just keep your eyes closed." The tall female technician patted Allie's leg as she drew herself straight in front of Allie, so that Allie could see her. "We're all through here. Someone will arrive soon to transport you back to ER."

Eyes watering, Allie squeezed them shut. In the distance, she heard several more voices.

The moment was surreal as once again she felt herself raised into the air. The sensation of floating surrounded her. She opened her eyes, but couldn't see who held her. Only the ceiling and light, colors of white and beige. There was a strong smell of antiseptic. The absolute trust she had to give to complete strangers would have driven her mad if her head didn't hurt so badly.

At least the first doctor she had seen said she didn't believe it was a serious injury. The MRI was to ensure that no internal or bone damage existed.

The wheels of the gurney she lay upon squeaked as someone pushed her down one hall and then the other. The motion and the blur of lights passing by sent a fresh wave of nausea through her. She gasped for a clean breath of air. At the same time, she heard a familiar voice.

"Alison Grant." It was Jake, and by his sharp tone he wasn't happy. "Where is she? Is she going to be all right?" The demand and concern in his voice was hard to miss.

"Jake." The minute she called his name, he was by her side. Or at least that's who she thought cupped her cold hands in his warm ones as the gurney pulled to a stop.

"Honey, how are you?"

She couldn't see him, feeling the grips of panic reaching out for her.

Moisture filled her eyes. "Jake, someone shot me." Just before they wheeled her in for a cat-scan Captain Jenson had told her she had been a victim of a drive-by shooting.

A shooting! She hadn't believed it at first. But when it finally sank in all she could think was that some sonofabitch had shot her. Tears streamed down her face, filling her ear.

"I know. Honey, please don't cry." Jake squeezed her hand.

She needed to see him. Know that it was really him by her side. “Kiss me.” The sudden appearance of his handsome face before her eyes was heartwarming. A lock of his dark hair fell forward. His soft lips touched hers ever so gently. “Don’t leave me.” Her bottom lip quivered.

His knuckles skimmed her cheek. “I won’t.”

“Uh. I need to get her out of the hall,” the orderly grumbled. She couldn’t see the man in charge of her gurney, but she knew immediately she didn’t like him.

“Don’t let go of my hand.” Her plea came out on a cry.

“I won’t,” Jake promised as the ceiling and lights began to flash by her. She closed her eyes to quiet the rumble in her stomach, as nausea struck her once again.

When her eyelids rose again, a dark-haired nurse was leaning over her. The woman smiled. Her foul breath made Allie hold hers. “Do you know where you are?”

Allie first instinct was to nod, but that was impossible. “Yes,” she gasped, catching another whiff of the nurse’s onion breath.

“Where?”

“Hospital. My name is Alison Grant, and I’ve been shot.” Allie’s words came out a little testier then she had planned, but she wanted her meeting with Ms. Badbreath to be short.

Allie couldn’t believe that someone had shot her.

“Good.” The woman moved out of Allie’s line of sight, and she sucked in a clean breath of air.

Allie could see the eye-rings of the curtain skid across the metal pole, making a hissing sound as it was whipped it back and someone stepped inside Allie’s makeshift room, before pulling the curtain closed. “You’re one lucky woman.”

Another familiar female voice stroked Allie's ears. It was Dr. Caldwell. She leaned forward and a weathered face came into Allie's view. "You have a three inch laceration. Bullet skimmed your head, but it didn't touch bone or matter. The bump on the back of your head would account for your lack of consciousness. A mild concussion. We'll keep you overnight for observation." The doctor disappeared from Allie's sight. She heard the swish of a pen across paper. "If everything checks out your husband can take you home tomorrow."

"Husband?" Had Jake told them he was her husband? "I want to go home *now*," Allie demanded, feeling the beat of tears against her eyelids.

"No, Allie." Jake's firm response held no room for discussion. She knew he was right. "I'll be with you the entire time. Tomorrow I'll take you home."

Allie heard the curtain slide across the pole twice. The doctor was gone. "Where are my clothes?"

He cocked a brow, bent and retrieved a plastic bag beneath her bed. As he rose, a sheepish expression slid across his face. He extracted her shredded clothing, holding them high so that she could see.

She gasped. "Those are my favorite jeans."

"Were your favorite jeans," he corrected.

"Well, shit." Her anger sparked a pain in her head and she grew quiet, trying to gather her composure. Jake set the clothes down, tucked the sheet around her tighter and then spread a warm blanket atop her.

The curtains rattled again and a police officer entered. "Miss Grant, I'm Officer Layton. I have a couple of questions to ask you about the incident." The man looked to be in his early twenties, blond hair peeking from beneath his cap and hardened brown eyes as he leaned over her. "Can you recall anything about the shooting?"

Allie caught herself before she shook her head. Instead, she said, "No. I stepped out of the house and headlights blinded me as I walked to my car. I can't remember anything else."

"Anyone mad at you or would like to see you harmed?"

A huff left Allie's lungs. "I've only been in the States for a couple of weeks, home for only a week. I've been working out of the country."

Of course, there were a host of scientists, her boss, and the entire pharmaceutical company not happy with her, but surely they wouldn't have anything to do with the shooting. She shared this information with the officer, before she said, "It had to be a random shooting."

"Ma'am, it's my experience that there are no random shootings. You may have been in the wrong place at the wrong time, but there is always a reason behind a shooting." Officer Layton asked a couple more questions before placing a business card in Allie's open palm. "If you remember anything else give me a call."

Allie tried to nod, but the brace held her immobilized. "Thank you."

Alone, Jake gently pressed his lips to hers.

The curtains swished opened. "Down, boy," the nurse hummed. "This young lady needs rest."

Laughter bubbled up in Allie's throat, but died quickly as pain rose with it.

"Keep your eyes on her, but your hands off," Mrs. Badbreath added gruffly, then winked at Allie. "Better get some sleep, honey. It's going to be a long night."

ꕥ

"Why do sick people go to hospitals? I could never understand that. Doctors and nurses poked and prodded me to the point sleeping was impossible." Allie hung on tight, cradled in his arms as he cautiously took one step at a time.

Jake was tired, still wearing the bloody T-shirt and shorts from last night. The look of distress on Allie's face when he had offered to pick up clean clothes for both of them had stopped him from leaving.

"Thank God, we're home." Allie released a sated sigh, before she asked another question. "Where are you taking me?" He headed the opposite way from her bedroom.

"My room and don't argue with me." Using his hip, he gave the door a nudge and it sprang open. He set her gently upon his bed, before disappearing into the bathroom.

He turned the faucet on and water splashed into the tub. He sat on the edge for only a moment making sure the temperature was right, not too cold—not too hot.

When he returned, she was sitting where he left her, picking at the caked blood on the side of her face that the nurse washing her had missed. Allie's hair was mussed, stiff from dry blood.

"I feel like crap." Her eyes were moist, a sadness making them appear wider. "Do I look as bad as I feel?"

He slipped a finger beneath her chin and smiled. "You're beautiful, Allie." It wasn't a lie. Even disheveled she was the sexiest woman he had ever laid eyes on.

A tear rolled down her face. "Liar. But thanks." A tremor shook her from head to toe. "I'm so tired of things going wrong. I feel dirty. I can't stand this blood all over me."

He reached for the tie at the back of her hospital gown and pulled. The back fell open revealing the smooth dip of her spine and the swell of her ass. “I know. Let me bathe you.”

“I can do it,” she insisted, gripping her gown as he tugged it off her shoulders.

“Let go, Allie.” He waited patiently for her to release the material. “You can’t get your wound wet. And the only way you’ll get your hair washed is if I help you.” Reluctantly, she moved her hand away. Jake pulled the gown from her body and tossed it aside. He lifted her into his arms and strolled across the room toward the bathroom.

“Ahhh...” she said as he lowered her into the tub. He turned off the water. It was deep enough that when she scooted downward it covered her shoulders. “This feels so good.”

Jake sat on the edge of the tub as she closed her eyes. He simply stared at her.

She was alive.

Unexpected anger and fear rose. As the blood dissolved, it turned the water pink. The odds that the cops would be able to identify the shooter were slim. Nothing like this had ever happened before in this neighborhood.

Why now?

Why Allie?

And if not Allie, then who? If the police were right someone in the neighborhood was being targeted.

Yellow crime scene tape still circled his yard. A police cruiser passed by. Officer Layton said they would make several passes throughout the next couple days just in case the perpetrator returned.

Jake could have lost Allie last night. The thought made his blood run cold. If he ever got his hands on the sonofabitch who did this to Allie, he'd kill him.

Jake pushed to his feet and retrieved a washcloth and a cup off the sink. Then he knelt beside the tub. Soap in one hand, he scrubbed it back and forth over the cloth, gently raised her leg, starting at her foot to wash her gently.

She gazed at him through sleepy eyes. "Thank you," she whispered, before closing her eyes once more.

With a tenderness he hadn't known he possessed, he cleansed her, one body part at a time. Washing her hair would be a challenge. She had a big bandage covering the wound on the left side of her head. He knew she wouldn't truly feel clean unless her hair was washed.

Tilting her head to the right, he used the cup to wet her hair. From the shampoo bottle on the counter, he squeezed a small amount of shampoo in his palms, rubbed them together, and then began to work it into her hair.

She moaned, soft and low. "That feels so good."

As he massaged her scalp, he accidentally touched the goose egg at the back of her head.

"Owww..." she cried out. Pain tightened her face.

His anger flared anew. "I'll kill the bastard," he growled.

Allie opened her eyes to mere slits. "You and I both know they'll probably never catch the guy. I can't believe this happened. *Here.* In our neighborhood."

"I don't want you going outside without me just in case the bastard returns." He started to run fresh water into the cup to wash the shampoo from her hair.

She gave a huff of disbelief. “That’s ridiculous. You don’t even know who the target is.” She yawned, the small action forcing a groan from her, making her face twist in pain.

“That’s true. But what’s to say that you won’t be in the wrong place at the wrong time again? I just want to be close.”

She gave him a weak smile.

After doing his best to rinse her hair without getting the bandage wet, he assisted her out of the bathtub. Using a large bath towel, he quickly dried her. There was a chill in the air and he didn’t want her getting cold, so he left her briefly and came back with his large white terrycloth bathrobe. It was far too big, as he bundled her up in it.

She looked like an imp, swallowed up in all that soft material. The image squeezed his heart. “Climb on the bed. I’ll get the blow-dryer.”

“You’re kidding, right? You’re going to actually dry my hair?” She giggled, crawling upon his large four-poster bed.

As he went back into the bathroom to fetch his blow-dryer, he cast a look over his shoulder, “You’ll catch a cold if you go to bed with wet hair.”

“Who told you that?”

He grabbed a brush while he was in the bathroom and moved back into the bedroom. “Your mom.”

Her brows pulled together in a confused expression.

“I stayed over from time to time when Mabel wasn’t feeling well.”

She shook her head gently. “You’ve been a good friend, Jake.”

Jake didn’t want to be just her friend. He wanted more—he wanted Allie.

"So what's going on between you and Leslie?" Allie's question stunned him into silence.

He shrugged, searching for the right words. "We saw each other occasionally when she was in town. Nothing serious."

"It appeared serious to Leslie." Allie searched his face.

"If there was something serious going on don't you think she'd have a key to the house? And do you think I would have had sex with you?"

Allie huffed. "I have a key to the house."

"Exactly," he said, hoping she understood.

Chapter Thirteen

Light burst through the parted curtains, spilling into the bedroom. It was morning and Allie wasn't alone. Spooned to her back was a very male and very naked Jake. His morning erection pressed tightly against her ass. She listened to him breathe, his soft snoring made her smile.

The dull ache in her head was gone. It had been almost a week since the shooting. The police hadn't discovered a thing. Thankfully no more incidents had occurred. She moved slightly and Jake's arm grew taut around her waist.

"Oh, no you don't," he mumbled sleepily. He tugged her closer to him.

She giggled. "Does that mean I can't get up and go to the bathroom?" The man had barely allowed her out of his sight or his bed, using the excuse it was easier to keep an eye on her.

"Hmmm... Okay, the bathroom and then you get right back in bed." He pushed into a sitting position. His dark hair stuck out in all directions.

She grinned, reaching for his bathrobe to cover her nakedness.

"What?" he asked, stretching and groaning.

Allie glanced at his hair, as she pushed her arms through the sleeves. "Rough night?"

He ran his palms across his hair, taming it into place. “No.” He returned her smile. “It was a great night. Well, except for the part where I fell asleep with a hard-on.”

She frowned. “Whose fault was that?” He had sworn no sex until after her doctor’s appointment today. It was a two-for-one visit. She’d make sure her head was screwed on tight and she wasn’t pregnant. She’d used the store bought test the other day and received a negative result, but a girl couldn’t be too careful.

Reaching for her, Jake pulled her into his arms. With the slightest of touches, he slid his lips across hers. He kissed her so softly she felt it deep within.

He cared.

That meant more to her than he would ever know. Day after day, he had taken care of her. Other than her mother, no one had ever made her feel so special.

He nuzzled her neck. His warm breath brushed across her skin. “Do you need help?”

The stubble on his face tickled as he trailed a path of kisses down her neck, in the hollow of her shoulder blade, heading down south to her breasts.

She laughed, pushing him away. “No, I think I can handle this one on my own.” After tossing one leg and then the other over the side of the bed, she pushed to her feet.

Vertigo hit hard.

She swayed, backing up, before she plopped down on the bed in a sitting position holding her head between her palms. Her stomach whirled as she tried to steady herself.

“You okay?” Jake asked as he moved to her side.

“I think I moved too fast.” She sucked in a deep breath, releasing it slowly. Little by little the nausea subsided.

He stroked her back, making small circles. "Do you want me to help you to the bathroom?"

"No. This is silly. I just moved too fast. I'm perfectly fine." Allie felt better today than she had in a while.

Palms pressed against the mattress, she gave it another go pushing into a standing position. A satisfied grin spread across her face, as she glanced over her shoulder. "See. Easy as cake." Barefoot, she padded across the cold floor and disappeared into the bathroom.

One look into the mirror confirmed what she had thought all along. "I look like shit." Her complexion was pale. Dark rings circled her eyes, making her wonder if she might be part raccoon. The white bandage was gone from her head, the laceration already beginning to scab, discoloring to a deep purple, which added nothing to her sex appeal. Oh, yeah. She couldn't forget waking Jake screaming last night, twice.

Her dreams were becoming more vivid—more frightening and fragmented.

Memories were flashes of jungle wildlife scattering into the thick vegetation, snapshots of faceless people, fire licking the sky. Smoke so heavy that it choked her, clashed with the musky scents of the rainforest.

And the screams.

Human and animal screams broke the silence. The crackle of flames, raging water, the thud of her own heartbeat and the pounding of feet felt as if they would forever echo in her ears. Strangely, she had dreamed of a waterfall.

In the middle of the night, she had awoken fighting the jungle, vines wrapped around her arms and legs, only to discover the bedding held her captive. It had taken her over an hour to fall back to sleep.

One thing Allie was sure of after her last nightmare—someone had been chasing her that evening in the jungle when her life changed.

It was almost laughable when she thought about it. "I survived an attack on the campsite, in the Amazon no less. A year with a tribe I couldn't communicate with. I get home and I'm shot in my own front yard."

"You okay in there?" Jake yelled from behind the door.

She leaned on the sink and gazed at her weary reflection in the mirror. "Yeah. Just talking to myself."

"You must have hit your head harder than the doctor thought." She could hear laughter in his voice.

"Ha ha. Funny man." She turned the water on cold, cupped it in her hands and splashed it on her face.

"Hey, I'm going to stir up something for breakfast."

"Food." Her stomach growled.

Allie turned the water off and grabbed a towel to dry her face. Jake's cologne sat on the counter. She picked it up and inhaled its fresh scent. In fact, the whole bathroom contained Jake's essence where once it had smelled like her mother—roses.

Jake had made his mark in every part of the house. This was his home now. Allie had to face the truth—like it or not.

Dammit. Agitation crawled up her arms. She refused to let this train of thought ruin her day. It was the first time since the shooting that she felt like her old self.

Allie ran her tongue over her teeth. *Yuck.* Well, almost like her old self.

The floor was cold beneath her bare feet as she padded out of the bathroom and through Jake's bedroom, down the hall, and into the other bathroom where her toothbrush was. Within seconds, she felt like a new woman. Fresh breath definitely made her feel better. She sucked in the cinnamon flavor that cooled her mouth as she headed for her bedroom.

Today she just wanted to relax. Shrugging out of her robe, she went to the dresser and retrieved a soft, over-sized T-shirt from the top drawer. She draped the shirt over her head, sight blocked for a brief moment. When she pulled it past her face, Jake stood before her. She startled, jerking the material down with a squeal.

"I liked you naked. And in my bed." The little growl in his voice slid up her spine, tightening the muscles in her stomach. Her nipples beaded with each of his words.

Jake closed the distance between them and took her into his arms. He captured her lips in a tender kiss, nibbled on her bottom lip, and caressed the corner of her mouth. All the while, he smoothed his hands up her thighs, grabbing the hem of her shirt and raising it slowly up her body. Before she knew it, she was as naked as he was.

He ran his tongue along the seam of her mouth. "Now don't you feel better?"

Allie leaned into his strong body, loving his taut muscles against her softness. "No," she lied.

He cupped her ass and squeezed. "You do this to me." His hard cock pressed into her belly. God, what she'd give to have him buried between her legs, moving in and out of her body. Just the thought dampened her thighs and sent tingles through her now heavy breasts.

She slipped her arms around his neck. "Take me to bed, Jake."

Achingly slow, he raised her in his arms. She tucked her legs around his waist, locking them at the ankles. His thick erection nudged her pussy. Wet and ready, she wiggled her hips and he easily slid deep inside her, filling her with such fullness.

"Jake." His name was a breathless moan. "Fuck me."

"We shouldn't." Even as he spoke, his hips moved, back and forth, driving in and out.

Allie loved the feel of her nipples rasping against the swirls of hair on his chest, loved the combination of spicy cologne and masculinity that screamed all male. Most of all she loved how he made her feel wrapped in his arms. All woman, and that she was the only one in his life. Even though it wasn't true, she reveled in the moment.

Her fingers wove through his hair, cupping his nape to pull him to her kiss. She traced his lips with her tongue, pushed gently. His mouth parted and she dipped inside to taste him. Coffee, mint toothpaste, and male.

"Allie," he whispered against her caress. She heard desire and need in his hoarse voice, the same desire and need that made her wet and slick as she rocked her hips in rhythm with his. "We shouldn't be doing this."

She nipped his bottom lip. "But we are."

He groaned, coarse and deep. "Not here. My room."

Wrapped in his arms, she held on tight as he carried her into the hall heading toward his bedroom. Entering, he went straight to the bed. He sat on the edge, slowly rolled onto his back, taking all her weight. Hands on her hips, he grinned. "Ride me."

She began a gradual pace, widening her thighs so that she felt every inch of him deep inside. The crown of his cock slid back and forth against her womb. The feeling was so incredible that her pussy tightened around him. The blood in her veins built to a simmering burn.

She laid her palms against his broad chest, her fingers pinching his nipples as she stared into his golden eyes.

His gaze flickered to the ceiling and she remembered the mirror that hung above them.

Men were so visual. Jake was no different.

He enjoyed watching her fuck him. It was in the gleam of his eyes, the way his breath hitched when she dragged her fingernails down his chest and then back up.

It was a complete and total turn-on.

When she tried to pick up the pace, his grip tightened and he stilled her hips. “Slow and easy. Honey, we shouldn’t even be doing this.”

“But I need you,” she whimpered.

His breath quivered as he pulled air deep into his lungs. He caressed a path across her abdomen to her breasts. He fondled and kneaded them, before pinching and pulling on her nipples.

“I need you too.” Concern wrinkled his forehead. “But I don’t want to hurt you.”

“You won’t,” she promised. Nothing short of an act of God would make her climb off him. “Please.” Her plea was a soft cry.

The hardness in his expression mellowed. “I can’t refuse you anything.” He stroked back her hair, pushing it behind an ear. “Do your worst, Allie Grant. Fuck me.”

She started to rock her hips when his hands on her hips drew her to a stop.

“Whoa, wait.” His body tensed. “No condom.”

Yikes. They had almost done it again.

In a fluid movement, he eased from beneath her and stood. Allie rolled to her side, watching him as he opened a bedstand drawer and shuffled through it. Within seconds, he had donned a sheath and crawled in beside her. He raised her and she straddled his hips like before.

"Where were we?" he asked, stroking her arms.

"I was just about to have my way with you." She angled her hips so that his cock pierced her slit. Little by little, he pushed deeper until seated completely. Then she began to sway back and forth, side by side, rotating her hips in small circles.

Jake's eyes darkened. His nostrils flared. "Ahhh..." The strangled sound came out on a groan.

He grasped her waist pushing her down hard upon his erection, as he thrust. His jaw clenched. The veins in his throat bulged. She felt the tremor that shook him.

"Come with me, Allie." His voice was breathless. He shoved a hand down where they joined, found her swollen clit and pressed.

Fire started at his fingertips, raced up her womb, spreading throughout her body. With each contraction, she jerked, writhing above him. She was hot. So hot inside that it felt like a wildfire was set free.

The gentleness in his touch was gone as he rolled her over on her back and pushed between her thighs.

As her climax continued to wash through her, she opened her eyes to see his taut ass in the mirror above. The sight was heady, muscles flexing and releasing, intensifying the heat spreading throughout her body. Their legs entwined, her fingernails scraping up and down his back, only fueled her orgasm.

A throaty sound rose from Jake as he came. The muscles across his shoulders and down his back bunched and released, reflecting in the mirror. He stilled, releasing a low sated growl, before he collapsed atop her.

The clench and release of her sex softly continued. His skin was warm against hers as they lay in each other's arms. She breathed in his masculinity mingling with the scent of sex in the air.

Heaven. Pure heaven.

Jake buried his head against her shoulder. He was quiet for a moment. "Have you used the test you bought last week?"

"What?" How did he know she had purchased a pregnancy test?

"I saw it on the car seat at the cemetery." He raised his head, leaning it against his palm to brace himself. Their eyes met.

"I did. It was negative."

He nailed her with an expression close to disappointment and then anger. "When were you going to tell me?"

Crap. Why hadn't she told him? And why had she felt a moment of discontent when she saw the results? "I'm sorry. I didn't think."

"Didn't think that I'd care?" She heard the hurt in his voice that spread to his eyes.

"No. I— Hell, I don't know why I didn't tell you." Things were getting complicated between her and Jake. She looked forward to lying beside him each night. Hungered for his touch, one he had withheld out of consideration and concern. "I killed a beautiful moment."

"Beautiful?" The hardness in his features disappeared.

She slapped him playfully on the chest. "Yeah. Beautiful."

It bothered Jake that Allie hadn't confided in him about the test results. Truth was he had begun to hope that she was pregnant. It was a selfish thought, but he couldn't help it.

Jake loved the way her blue eyes twinkled. Hell. He loved everything about her.

"You're beautiful." He leaned down and gave her a quick peck on the cheek. "Now sausage or bacon?"

"Sausage." She lowered her eyelashes and her voice. "Nice big sausage."

Laughter burst from his mouth. He rolled over on his side and off the bed.

She frowned, growing quiet.

Damn, he knew he had to ask the question even if he dreaded the possible answer. "What's wrong?"

Her bottom lip disappeared between her teeth. She bit the corner of her lip, before she asked, "Do you really think it was a random drive-by?" Wariness weighed heavy in her eyes, it etched creases into her forehead and wiped away the smile that had brightened her face only minutes ago.

"It had to be." He tried to reassure her. "It was bad timing. It could have happened to anyone." Yet it hadn't happened to anyone. It had happened to Allie and clearly, she was frightened.

"Arghhh..." she growled, throwing up her hands in an air of defeat. "I hate feeling helpless—scared." He heard unshed tears in her voice. "I've felt this way for so long."

A year lost in the jungle with people she couldn't communicate with had to have been difficult. Now this.

He leaned into her and hugged her close. "You're home, Allie, and everything will be okay. You're safe with me."

"Thank you, Jake." She blinked hard, fighting the moisture welling in her eyes. "Guess I lost it for a moment. You're right; everything will be just fine. How about that breakfast?" Her smile looked a little too tight to be genuine.

"Breakfast it is." His feet thumped on the wood floor, as he crossed the room. He reached the door as the telephone next to the bed started to ring. He turned just in time to see her naked body stretch along with her arm to reach the receiver. Placing it to her ear, she said, "Hello," repeating herself several times, before she hung up the telephone.

"Who was it?" Jake asked.

"Another heavy breather," she replied, but this time concern darkened her expression. The telephone calls were coming more frequently now. Perhaps it was time to tell the police about the calls.

Chapter Fourteen

It was a celebration.

Allie raised the glass of wine to her lips and took a sip. She appeared to be back to normal. The doctor had given her a series of tests, which included balance, movement and reflexes. She had passed them without any difficulty.

Better yet, she wasn't pregnant.

The mall was busy. The packed restaurant where they dined hummed with voices, but Jake's was the only one she heard.

"After Mom died I used my inheritance to start my own business." Deep and sexy, his words smoothed across her skin like silk, making her nipples harden to sensitive peaks against her satin bra and red, cotton shirt she wore. She tugged at the collar, feeling the heat of her skin against the back of her hand.

Had his voice always been this captivating?

He slipped a piece of cheesecake between his lips. She watched him chew, remembering how that same mouth had pleasured her earlier this day.

Had he always had the most kissable lips?

Muscles rippled beneath his black polo shirt. She had the incredible urge to slip it over his head and trace her fingers over every sinewy one of them. Next to go would be his black jeans.

"There was just enough left over for the down payment on the house," he continued.

"Why didn't you purchase the house you grew up in?" Her question made him sit a little straighter. The fork he held clinked against his plate. She could see the look in his eyes that screamed *here we go again*. Yet, that wasn't how she'd meant it. It had simply been a question.

Jake cleared his throat. "Your house was more home than mine ever was."

It was true. Almost every childhood memory she had Jake was in it. She hadn't seen his parents around much. They were always gone on business, leaving Jake a latchkey child.

The sweet scent of pastries baking reminded Allie that several times Jake's parents had forgotten his birthday. Her mom had been the one to bake him a cake. Together her mother and she had sung "Happy Birthday" to Jake.

Had he suffered?

Mentally Allie shook her head. What was happening? Jake was bewitching her. Little by little, he was taking over her thoughts, wrapping himself around her heart. Like when they were kids, he was always there—always touching her in some small way. Whether it was the red roses he brought her yesterday, or simply the way he warmed her feet at night with his own. Perhaps it was the way he held her so tenderly or how he made her body burn when they made love.

He was becoming a habit she didn't want to break.

Jake laid his hand over hers. "You okay?"

Not to mention, the man was insightful. He saw everything.

"You're not eating." He glanced down at her apple pie. A piece of Dutch apple she hadn't taken more than two bites of.

"Full." Over the past year, food had been scarce in the Amazon. Her appetite hadn't yet returned.

From his pocket, he extracted his wallet and pulled his credit card out. "I need to get a few things while we're here. In the mood to go shopping?"

Not really, but she said, "Sure."

Shopping was dangerous for a woman who needed to hold onto her money since she had no job, which reminded her she had to call Brayer Tech. Enough was enough. She needed the question of employment settled.

After the dark-headed waitress finished ogling Jake and returned with his credit card, they rose. Immediately, he took Allie's hand. It felt so right to walk hand-in-hand as they wandered into the mall.

A boy around the age of three ran into Jake's jeans-clad leg. He released her hand to steady the youngster and heaved the child into his arms. "Hey, buddy. Where's your mother?"

Before the boy could answer, a frantic woman in her early twenties came around the corner yelling, "Kyle."

The boy in his arms squirmed, jutting out his finger. "There her is."

Relief spread across the short, blonde-haired woman's face, as she ran toward her son. "Oh dear God." She jerked the child out of Jake's arms and hugged the boy, so tightly he cried out, "Mommy."

"Don't you ever run off again." She looked up at Jake. "Thank you. I only turned my back for a moment."

Jake gave her one of his prize-winning smiles. "No problem." Gazing back at the boy, he dipped his finger beneath the child's chin. "Mind your mama."

The woman thanked Jake once more and moved on. Footsteps in sync, Allie's and Jake's boots clunked across the marble floor.

Once again, Jake took Allie's hand in his. "Come on. There's a Frederick's of Hollywood in this mall."

She gazed up at him. It was amazing how comfortable Jake had been with the child. Someday he would make a great father. The fatherly image vanished as he pulled her into a store with decadent clothing.

Jake took a leather corset off the rack and held it to his nose. "Leather." His eyes closed, as he inhaled deeply. His sexy expression when he looked at Allie warmed her blood. "You need this."

Allie froze. She didn't have the money for such a frivolous thing. "Jake, I—"

"No arguing. My treat." He chose a leather thong to match.

"May I suggest the fishnet stockings and matching fingerless gloves?" A salesclerk came up from behind, making Allie whirl around. The middle-aged woman smiled sweetly. In her hands, she held the sinful accessories.

"We'll take those and the little red teddy in the window," Jake added, gazing about the store. "I like those shoes, too." He pointed to a pair of patent leather caged sandals with five-inch heels. "In black, red too."

"Jake—"

"Let me do this." He pulled her into his arms. "I'm getting hard just thinking about you in those shoes," he whispered for her ears only. The evidence of his arousal pressed firmly to her belly. "You have beautiful legs, Allie. But your breasts drive me wild."

What could she say?

The man was a sweet-talker.

His sensual words made her hot all over. Her breasts felt heavy with need, while moisture dampened her panties and jeans. She wanted him here—now.

Allie waited until the clerk wasn't looking. Discreetly she rubbed her body against his cock, forcing a low growl from Jake.

"Not fair," he mumbled.

"And you are?" Allie laughed, before her tone softened. "Take me home, Jake."

ꙮ

The packages slipped from Jake's arms and landed on the living room floor as Allie pulled him to her. She kissed him as if she were starving for his touch. Her hands were everywhere, tearing at his clothing, stripping his shirt from his chest, as her fingers worked feverishly at releasing the button of his jeans.

He tried to undress her, but she moved his hands out of the way, stepping backward. "No." Heat simmered in her blue gaze. "I'm calling the shots this evening."

Jake laughed on a breath. She was so damn cute.

He'd never let a woman take control or yield a whip over him. Still he couldn't help wondering what it would feel like to be at Allie's mercy.

Hell. Wasn't he already? She'd already stolen his heart.

He loved the woman—always had.

"Take your boots off," she demanded, already getting into character.

Without a word, he jerked one black boot and then the other off. Socks removed, he stood quietly to await her next command.

With a drop-dead expression that made his cock jerk with anticipation, she approached him. Her warm fingertips smoothed up his arm, caressing his chest. “Strip.” Her voice was a lightning strike of adrenaline in his veins, hot and exciting.

Devilment rose in her eyes, as she slid her hand across his chest and pinched his nipple.

His breath caught. Desire slammed into his gut hard. His dominant nature raced to the surface. His palms itched to feel her beneath him. He flexed then clenched his hands. He wanted to be the one who stripped her naked, took control, bent her over the couch and fucked her from behind.

“Honey, I don’t know if this is going to work.”

Determination was in her stance. Instead of giving in, she increased the pressure on his nipple, sending rays of fire through his chest that shot straight for his groin.

“Strip,” she repeated firmly. Her unwavering glare was so fiery he quickly unzipped his jeans, hooked his thumbs in the waistband of his shorts and pushed them to his ankles.

Female appreciation scanned his length. “Nice,” she hissed. With a snap of her wrist, she slapped his ass. The sharp sting was something he had never experienced, but he had to admit it inflamed him more.

Stepping away from him, she folded her arms over her chest, which rose and fell rapidly. She was as aroused as he was. The knowledge made him harden more.

“Now get up those stairs.” She slapped him again on the ass and the sweet pain fueled his desire. But when she said, “Wait for me on the bed,” he groaned. The gleam in her gaze was undoing him. The role play was turning her on. He could scent her excitement in the air.

Holy shit. He wasn't going to make it that far. He wanted Allie and he wanted her now. "Allie—"

She jabbed a finger in the direction of the stairs, trying to look tough, but the twinkle in her eyes stole the impact she attempted to portray.

Her playful mood was more than he could ask for. He bowed his head so she couldn't see the grin that swept across his face. Taking the steps two at a time, he bounded up the stairs not knowing what to expect—anticipating every moment.

By the time he walked through the open bedroom door, his erection throbbed and his imagination was running away with him. Just what did the little minx have in mind?

Handcuffing?

Whipping?

The velour comforter was soft against Jake's backside as he lay upon the bed. Minutes ticked by. Where was she?

He glanced at himself in the mirror above. Without a second thought, he took himself in hand. Fingers closing around his shaft, he slid his palm up to the crown and back down. The picture reflecting down at him was wicked. This time his hips rose to greet his stroke.

"Uh-uh-uh."

He snapped his head around to see Allie leaning against the doorjamb dressed in the little red teddy and the stiletto heels he had purchased for her earlier.

"No touching yourself." Her perky nipples pressed against the silky material, every inch of her visible through the translucent cloth. As he expected, the stilettos made him horny as hell.

Jake's pulse leaped into second gear. His heart pounded. She was so sexy his grip tightened around his cock. "Doesn't it turn you on to watch me pleasure myself?"

She ignored him, but he knew the truth. Watching someone masturbate was fucking hot.

Her heels clicked across the floor, heading toward his box of treasures. "Release yourself, or you'll be punished."

He raised a brow, a smile touching his lips. "Punished?"

She glanced over a shoulder and nodded. "Punished." Her wheaten hair was loose, falling around her shoulders. Her slender legs were a feast for his eyes. "Don't make me whip you."

Back facing him, her legs shoulder-width, she bent over to retrieve something from the box, giving him a bird's eye view of her tender flesh through her crotchless panties.

Jake sucked in another breath, holding back the urge to go to her and take her from behind or maybe lick his tongue across her moist slit, again and again.

Allie pivoted holding his red furry handcuffs and ankle bracelets and several strips of Velcro in her hands. A seductive smile on her face, she slinked toward him, each step sexier than the one before.

Silently, she attached a strip of Velcro around one of the four posters of the bed, then reached for his hand. The fleece of the handcuff was soft around his wrist as she attached it to the post. One after another, she secured his wrists and ankles, until he was spread-eagle before her.

The cool evening air was chilly, fading fast as the heat in his body soared.

The wicked image in the mirror above him made his skin burn. It would be easy to break his bondage, but no way in hell would he do it. Liquid excitement pumped through his veins as he watched her walk back to the box. He was dying to see what she'd do next.

Confusion pulled her brows together. "What's this?" In her palm, Allie held a controller, dangling from her finger was a jelly-soft support ring.

"A Triple Action Pleasurizer." His only cock toy and it was the first thing that had drawn her.

"How do you use it?" she asked, stretching it and then letting it spring back into shape.

"It's goes around a man's balls. Inside those two slits at each end are small vibrators, called bullets. One energizes the triple prong to pleasure you, the other activates the special nodule to pleasure me."

"Really?" A mischievous twitch pulled at the corner of her mouth. "We might need that a little later." The next thing she extracted was his mammoth dildo and a tube of lubricant.

Jake immediately tensed. His fingers curled into fists. "Don't even think about it."

She wouldn't dare.

The joyful snicker that bubbled up from her throat was priceless. The little wench was teasing him and having a blast judging by her grin. Still he didn't take an easy breath until she placed the dildo down and instead picked up some climax beads and a condom.

On a whim, he had purchased the one-time use beads guaranteed to make climaxes strong and powerful. The string contained four small balls at different intervals. He had yet to try them and never had intended them for himself. The gleam in Allie's heavy gaze told him he would get the opportunity.

Silently, she went back to rustling through the chest. Her gaze jerked to his. Her eyes darkened with concern, she frowned, dangling a silk noose from her finger.

Holy shit! What must she be thinking?

"It's not what you think. I don't go for asphyxiation. I got that as a gag-gift at Halloween."

She released a heavy breath, dropped the rope and smiled.

With sleek, sensuous movements, she crawled upon the bed, the beads, lubricant, condom, and cock ring in her hand. Eyelashes half-shuttered, she stroked his body with enough heat he felt the sizzle across his skin. As she neared, the smell of lilies and her woman's musk made him tug at his restraints.

He wanted to touch her.

When she climbed between his thighs, the silk of her teddy tickled his legs and sent a rush of blood to his balls, filling them with an ache. Silently, she lubed the beads.

His anus puckered. The muscles in his legs grew tight. A wave of unease filtered through him. So this is what his partners felt.

"Allie—"

She stole his objection away when she placed a dab of the cool lubricant against his tight entrance. Her finger gently nudged his ass.

Man, did he have to admit that felt good?

Oh, how the tables had turned. He almost laughed at the irony. He had always dreamed of Alison Grant handcuffed to his bed; instead, he was.

The first bead felt strange, generating a slight sting as she eased it inside him. The burn quickly disappeared replaced with anticipation for the next bead. The tip of her tongue smoothed across her lips, then she leaned down and licked a path around the crown of his shaft. Her eyes were dark pools of desire as she rose. She pushed another bead deep inside him.

It was amazing.

He had heard the anal cavity was one of most sensitive areas, especially for a man. If he shifted his hips just right, he could swear the little bead stroked his prostate gland, sending a shiver throughout.

Every muscle in Jake's body drew tight. Ankles and wrists bound, he fisted his fingers, when what he really wanted to do was take his cock into his hands and stroke.

Before long, all four round objects were lodged up his ass. The protruding string was a small irritant sliding around as he puckered and released his ass to get the full sensation of the beads.

Allie's palms smoothed up and down his thighs, one hand disappearing between his legs. "Do you like that?" She gave a little tug on the string.

The pressure against his tight entrance from the inside out was amazing. Fire raced down his cock, curling his toes. He sucked in a breath to hold back the inevitable climax.

"*Uh-uh-uh.* No coming until I give you permission." Even as Allie spoke, she wrapped her hand around his engorged erection and began to stroke. Up and down, she teased him into a sexual frenzy. He tried not to thrust, but his hips had a mind of their own, slamming back and forth into her touch. He glanced up at the mirror, watching his cock slip through her fingers.

His body tensed. One more stroke and he was a goner.

Jake held his breath, waiting for the moment of unadulterated pleasure that never came as she released her grip.

Raising his hips to meet thin air, he groaned, "Ah...come on, honey. Finish it."

But she was already off the bed, searching through his box for something else to torment him with. Her back to him, she slipped off her red teddy, leaving only her crotchless panties and five-inch stilettos to adorn her body.

She turned with a flogger in her hand.

"Fuck." It was all he could say. She was a vision of naughtiness, sexy and wanton, as she snapped the leather thongs through the air. Her nipples were pebbled, her breasts full and inviting.

Her heels clicked on the wood flooring as she stepped forward. "What do you want, my precious boy toy?"

Boy toy?

Another step brought her closer. "Do you want me to whip or fuck you?"

"Fuck me," he answered without hesitation.

"Hmmm...I don't think so." She dragged the cool thongs of the flogger across his chest, down his abdomen, to whisper softly across his groin.

"Oh God," he moaned, throwing back his head. "I need you now, Allie."

"How much?" A flick of her wrist, the laces of the whip bit into his thigh.

"So much it hurts." Man, did it hurt. His erection was rigid, just the mere caress of the flogger across his tender flesh sent waves of pleasure-pain to pulsate in his balls.

Allie tossed the flogger aside. Her throat muscles tightened. Her breathing elevated as she climbed upon the bed. Instead of crawling atop him, taking him deep inside her, she reached for the condom. Within no time, she sheathed him. Next, she reached for the cock ring. Her hands shook while easing the jelly-ring over his erection, placing the nodule where his testicles and cock met. Only then did she straddle him, angling her hips so that her body accepted his.

The word *heaven* came to mind as her warm, wet slit parted allowing him to thrust deep inside her. She pressed her hips tightly to his. In seconds, he felt a vibration that rocked him down to his core.

"Oh my," she cried out breathlessly. He knew the two rubber prongs were against her clit. One hand pressed against his chest, holding her upright, while her other hand disappeared behind her. The slight tug against his anus said she had found the string to the climax beads.

Every muscle and tendon in his body clenched. Back and forth, she rode him hard, driving him closer and closer to ecstasy, as the vibration of the cock ring continued to stimulate.

With a firm jerk, he pulled against his restraints. The Velcro made a ripping sound as they released.

His hands were free.

Immediately, he gripped her hips, holding her to him as he began to thrust wildly.

The heat in his body soared. He dug his fingers deeper into her tender flesh. Electricity arced between them and then exploded.

A hoarse cry met his.

A streak of lightning raced up his cock, as Allie tore the beads from his body, igniting the nerve endings inside him.

The bed shook beneath Jake.

He couldn't breathe.

His entire body was a mass of sensation. Fire and ice. Wild and fiery, flames engulfed him. He tried to speak, but all that came from his throat was a strangled groan.

Never had he felt anything like this before.

Allie whimpered. Her face was flushed, her body went boneless. She leaned forward, falling against his chest. He wanted to wrap his arms around her, hold her close, but he didn't have the strength to move. Whatever she had done to him had drained him completely.

Small spasms continued to milk his cock, until finally she lay quiet atop him.

When he was able to move, he embraced her, the handcuffs trailing across her skin. *"I love you,"* was on the tip of his tongue, but he withheld the words, content with just being near her.

The moment was blissful, until the telephone on the dresser beside the bed erupted.

"You're on top. You have to answer it," he said, pressing his lips to her neck.

She giggled softly, tilting her head to give him more access. "I don't have the energy."

The telephone rang persistently.

"All right." He rolled her off him, fumbling for the receiver, before pressing it to his ear. "Hello."

"May I speak with Alison?" the husky male voice requested.

A wave of anxiety slammed into Jake, as he handed Allie the telephone. "It's for you." The caller had the tone of a friend, not someone intent on addressing a business issue.

"Hello." A long pause followed. She frowned. "Hello." Her worried gaze met his and then she froze.

"Allie?"

She dropped the receiver.

"Allie, what's wrong?"

Her bottom lip trembled. "He said, 'You're a dead woman'."

Chapter Fifteen

Allie cried out, jerking into a sitting position and fighting the sheets tangled around her body. Her pulse raced. Her heart threatened to burst from her chest. She blinked away tears and the last vision of the nightmare.

Patches of broken memories rose, only to die in her mind. Running. Screams. Flames reaching like ominous fingers into the sky. She could smell the heavy scent of smoke. Pain. Raging waters, the waterfall, and then darkness, but not before her faceless assailant appeared.

She hugged herself tightly. Each night her nightmares became more vivid—more twisted. She wasn't sure anymore what was real.

Not to mention the damn mirror above her was becoming disconcerting. Every move she made reflected, catching her eyes. At times, it scared the shit out of her. The telephone calls were coming more frequently, always heavy breathing and a muffled threat. Each time the calls came from a different telephone booth around the city. There was no way for the police to track her tormentor, nor her shooter. She and Jake were on edge. He had even gone as far as insisting she not step outside the house without him.

"This is absurd." Allie hated how insecure she felt. "It has to stop now."

With determination, she pushed from the bed and stood, stretching her naked frame to work out the muscle kinks.

Pop.

Snap.

"Oh, that feels good." Allie looked around what used to be her mother's bedroom.

Each night she fell asleep in Jake arms. He made her feel safe—loved. With Jake by her side, she didn't feel quite as alone or lost.

Nothing about the ownership of the house came up. Neither one of them seemed to want to go there. She had come to grips that he owned the house.

This morning Jake had left for work just before sunrise. She had seen concern in his eyes as he kissed her goodbye. He worried about her and that comforted Allie.

Stepping inside her bedroom, she went to her dresser and pulled open a drawer, retrieving a thong, bra, and socks. As she slipped them on, she pondered on all that had happened—how her life had changed—and where to go from here.

Yesterday she received a call from her previous employer. She slammed the drawer shut. Dan Grover, human resources, had announced, "Your services are no longer required." She was still fuming.

Next drawer down, she chose a pair of soft blue jogging pants and matching jacket. Was Brayer refusing to renew her contract while she remained under investigation? The nice severance package Grover offered would probably disappear should they find any evidence to implicate her in the attack on the facility in the Amazon. At least now she had a little more money to give her time to decide where she wanted to go from here.

Allie couldn't believe they thought she was involved. Jake had contacted a lawyer friend. Lawrence Davison was looking into her case.

She crammed one leg into the pants followed by the other. She was out of a job and out of a home. She pulled them up to her waist, slipping on a T-shirt and then the jacket, before hunting down her tennis shoes and putting them on.

The soles of her shoes squeaked across the floor as she left her bedroom, headed down the hall, and descended the stairs. Her steps were filled with determination. She stomped through the living room, threw open the curtains, and pushed the window open.

Jake had been listening to the radio this morning before he left. The perfect morning promised by the weatherman had come to fruition. There wasn't a cloud in the sky. For a moment, she watched a hawk soar on the gentle breeze high above the rooftops.

Next door, Mr. Wilson was mowing his yard. Several children rode their bikes down the street. Black birds chirped, flittering about in the bare branches of a maple tree. In the distance, she heard dogs barking.

Allie pulled in a breath of air, inhaling the scent of fresh-mowed grass and sunshine. She would give anything to feel its warmth on her skin.

Yet the thought of stepping a foot outside made her heart pound, something close to fear squeezed her chest.

"You're being silly," she chastised herself. "It's daylight. What the hell could happen?"

A heavy sigh forced her shoulders to rise and fall.

The whish-whish-whish of the sprinkler system in Ms. Tatum's yard caught her attention. The elderly woman had beautiful lilies—yellow, white, and deep purple.

Two boys about the ages of seven to nine rode their bikes in front of the house, their feet peddling as fast as they could. Behind them on a small pink bike was a girl about four frantically trying to keep up.

"Wait for me," the dark-haired girl shouted just before her front tire nipped the curb and threw her into air. She landed hard upon the sidewalk.

Allie didn't think twice—she simply reacted.

Racing to the door, she threw it open and burst outside, heading for the child who was now lying on the concrete crying. As she reached the child, she saw the boys were nowhere in sight. Mr. Wilson was preoccupied with his mower, his back facing them.

"Are you all right?" Allie asked as she knelt, helping the girl to a sitting position.

Big blue eyes moist with tears looked up at Allie. "My knee." The child's brown pants were scuffed and torn. Through the slit in the material, Allie could see red angry road rash. "I want Matt. Where's Matt?"

Allie pushed back the girl's soft hair, tucking it behind her ear. "Sweetie, I don't know where he is. Where do you live?"

She sniffled, pointing down the street.

"Dawn!" The eldest of the two boys yelled as they rounded the corner. His feet pumped even faster than before toward Allie and the girl. Anxiously, he jumped off his bike. The other boy skidded his tires to a stop.

Dawn puckered up and began to wail.

Wide-eyed, the boy Allie assumed was Matt looked almost panicky. "Mom's going to kill me for letting her get hurt."

Allie picked Dawn up in her arms. "Shhh…"

"Is she okay, lady?" Matt asked, rising to stand.

"Yeah. She's just scared and she scraped her knee." It took a moment but soon the child stopped sobbing.

"Here," Matt held out his arms, "I'll take her home." Allie released Dawn into his arms. The little girl smiled, clinging to his neck. "Thanks." With his sister in his arms, he started walking down the street.

"What about the bikes?" his friend asked.

"Leave 'em. We'll come back for them."

Allie headed back to the house when Jake's red truck pulled into the driveway. She waved and he frowned. In no time, he was out of the vehicle and by her side.

His gaze quickly scanned the area. "What are you doing outside?" He slid his palms over the front of his white coveralls and then reached for her. She went willingly into his arms. From the corner of her eye, she caught the smile on Mr. Wilson's weathered face as he knelt and pulled a weed.

"Easy, Jake. I just helped a little girl who wrecked on her bike." She gazed up at Jake, seeing worry lines crease his forehead.

"Where?" he growled.

"Her brother took her home."

He gave her a look of disbelief.

"For goodness sake, there are their bikes." She pointed to the two bikes lying in the street by the curb. "What are you doing home?" The words came so easily to Allie she paused. This arrangement was getting way too comfortable.

"Forgot my wallet." Plaster spackled his clothes and his hands. She plucked a couple pieces of the white chalky stuff off his cheek. "Why don't you come to work with me?" he asked.

"I don't think so." She patted him on the chest. "I'll be fine."

"I don't like this, Allie."

"You're being silly. Since I'm already outside I thought I'd walk to the end of the street and back. Okay?"

He hesitated, as if he thought to argue with her. He scanned up and down the street. "Okay." He agreed, but didn't release her. Finally, he did and headed for the house. Before he stepped inside, he turned and said, "To the end of the street and back."

She shook her head, laughing. "Yes, sir."

Pulling one knee to her chest and then the other, she began to stretch. She did several leg lunges, then hastily walked down the driveway to the sidewalk. Noticing that her shoe was untied, she bent just as she heard the door to the house open and shut.

As she stood, the squeal of tires made her spin around to see a black sedan barreling down the street. It steered off to the right, straight for Allie.

She froze.

Couldn't speak—couldn't breathe.

Everything happened at once.

Mr. Wilson screamed, "Watch out!"

From somewhere behind her she heard Jake yell her name.

The car ran over the two children's bikes, before jumping the curb and popping into the air. Metal twisted and moaned the second the tires landed on the sidewalk and skidded toward her. The smell of burning rubber followed.

Allie felt the brush of death breeze by her as someone grabbed her arm. The sharp sudden jerk had her flying through the air and landing hard against an unyielding body.

The fender missed her by only a fraction of space.

At the same time, the car tore through the front yard, tires flinging grass and dirt; barely missing her mother's rosebushes, before it fishtailed off the sidewalk and spun down the street.

Cold fear iced Allie's veins, chilling her to the bone. She trembled in the warm arms that held her.

In the distance, feet pounded against the pavement growing louder as people neared. Voices rose, becoming a roar of white noise that threatened to drown her.

Eyes squeezed shut, darkness closed in on her.

"Breathe." Jake gave her a little shake and her mouth opened upon a gasp. He brought them both into a sitting position on the grass, then eased her onto his lap.

"Jake." Her fingers dug into his coveralls, clinging to him. Tears fell down her cheeks.

He stroked her back in small, gentle circles. "Don't cry, honey." He pressed his chin against the top of her head. "Did anyone get the license number?"

"Four, five two, D-A-M." Mr. Wilson leaned forward. "Weren't no accident. Aimed straight at our Allie," he whispered for Jake's ears only, but Allie heard every word and their implication.

Someone was definitely trying to kill her.

A crowd was gathering. Once again, his quiet neighborhood had been shaken.

Allie was eerily quiet as Jake stood and gathered her into his arms and headed for the house. Mr. Wilson and Ms. Tatum, the elderly neighbor across the street, followed them inside the house. Ms. Tatum was on her cell telephone with the police.

"I was watching from my living room window. Raced down the street like a bat out of hell and narrowed right on the girl."

Ms. Tatum scowled, pulling her gray brows together. "No. I said she wasn't hit."

Jake laid Allie down on the couch, kneeling beside her. He held her hand in his. "You okay, honey?"

She stared at him, confusion clouding her eyes. "Why me?"

He pushed his free hand through his hair. "I don't know."

Mr. Wilson offered Allie a glass of water. Why did people always run for a glass of water in an emergency? Did water have some magical property that calmed the nerves? And why was he thinking of that at a time like this?

Allie took the glass, giving the man a polite "thank you" before she turned back to Jake. "Why?"

He had no answer for her. Instead, he shrugged and shook his head.

Ms. Tatum drew the lightweight quilt off Mabel's recliner and spread it over Allie. "Anything I can do for you, sweetie?"

"No. Thank you, Ms. Tatum." Allie's voice was weak, fragile.

Ms. Tatum pulled on Jake's sleeve, nudging him to his feet. He stood off to the side with the woman. "Police are coming. Damnedest thing, boy. What's going on?"

"I wish I knew." He patted the old woman on the hand, trying to ease the concern in her tired eyes.

A loud rapping noise brought all their gazes to the front door. They stood unmoving for just a second, before Jake walked over, peered through the peephole, and opened it wide.

Two uniformed cops stood before them. Officer Layton, the policeman who had followed them to the hospital the night Allie was shot, stood beside another officer who was at least a foot taller than him. His badge reflected the name Boyle.

"Officer Boyle." He shook Jake's hand. "Officer Layton." Jake took the man's hand.

"We've met," he said, looking Layton straight in the eyes. "I don't think it was a random shooting."

"What happened?" the officer asked.

Jake led them into the living room and offered them each a chair, which they didn't take. Instead, the officers went different directions. Officer Boyle stepped into the kitchen with Mr. Wilson and Ms. Tatum, while Officer Layton began to ask Jake and Allie questions.

Allie went into as much detail as she could about where she'd been the last year and about the attack against the pharmaceutical company in the Amazon. And she couldn't forget about the telephone calls.

As Jake contacted his crew to inform them he wouldn't be returning to the job site, the officer contacted his station.

"Four, five two, delta, alpha, mega," Officer Layton said into his shoulder radio. His head cocked at an unnatural angle. "Black sedan, possibly an older Cadillac, maybe 2003."

That was Jake's best guess.

Officer Layton waited patiently for a response. The radio squawked. The woman's voice on the other end grew quiet. "The vehicle was reported stolen approximately two hours ago," the officer said.

Jake felt the tendons in his neck tense. "This just keeps getting better." He sat beside Allie, pulling her into his arms. "So what do we do?"

"I'll write up a report and the case will be handed over to a detective. You should be contacted shortly," Officer Layton said as Officer Boyle and the rest joined her.

"What do I do until then?" Allie wrung her hands.

"Stay alert. Report any suspicious individuals," Officer Boyle recommended.

"We'll have patrol cars swing by the neighborhood for the next couple of days," Officer Layton added. "Until this perp is apprehended it's probably best if you limit your outside activities. Change your routine."

"That's all the help you can offer her?" Ms. Tatum snarled at the officers. The elder woman had spunk.

"We don't have the manpower or the funds to assign one-on-one protection," Officer Boyle explained. "It's not like television."

"Christ sakes. The girl is in danger," Ms. Tatum rebutted.

The officers gave a couple more suggestions before they left. Mr. Wilson and Ms. Tatum followed the officers out the door.

Finally, Jake and Allie were alone. The hands of the clock said one o'clock.

"Want me to call for pizza?" he asked.

She pulled the quilt up around her shoulders and shook her head. "I'm not hungry." He saw the shiver that passed through her.

"How about a movie?"

"Whatever." She dragged in a heavy breath, before her backbone straightened. She raised her chin slightly. "Yeah. Let's go to the movies."

He pointed to the television. "I meant TV." There was no way in hell she was leaving this house.

She threw back the quilt and stood. "This is ridiculous. I can't hide away in this house." Grass and dirt stained her once-clean jogging suit. "If I do—he wins." Her gaze narrowed.

He didn't like the fight that burned in her eyes. "Allie, maybe you should lay low."

A very unladylike growl rose. Her jaw tightened. "I've laid low for days." She clenched her fists.

Fear had switched to anger.

Jake wasn't sure which one he preferred, but Allie's anger was always a force to reckon with.

She glanced down at her dirty clothing. "I need to change." She made her way quickly to the stairs.

"Wait." He trailed after her. "Let's talk about this."

"Nothing to talk about." She bounded up each step. When she reached the top, she spun around. "I can't let him possess me." Moisture brightened her blue eyes, but didn't fall. "I've lived in fear for the past year not knowing who I am, whether I'd ever make it back home. Whoever is stalking me did this to me. I'm sure. I'll remember what happened in the jungle someday." Her voice lowered. "And then the sonofabitch will pay."

Now all Jake had to do was keep her alive.

Chapter Sixteen

Allie fidgeted in the cushiony chair, her fingernails biting into the armrests as she crossed and uncrossed her legs. Unable to relax, she finally settled with the soles of her tennis shoes squarely on the floor next to Jake's boots. The scent of buttery popcorn, hot dogs too long on the grill, and candy turned her stomach. She felt nauseous, not to mention a fool. Jake had tried for three hours to convince her that leaving the house was a bad idea, but she had held fast to her decision, until now.

How stupid was it to court danger?

Instead of lying low, she sat in a darkened theater giving her stalker just the right venue to attack again.

Dumb. Dumb. Dumb.

She was tired of feeling like a victim. All she wanted was to take control of her life. Was that too much to ask?

Jake wasn't happy with her. The fact that he had insisted on sitting in the very last row, backs to the wall and close to an exit, revealed his uneasiness. Add to that the small detail that he had yet to watch the screen. His head was in constant motion scanning the room.

Both of them sitting on the edge of their seats, neither one of them had paid attention to the previews. Only the deafening roar of the surround sound shaking the walls told them the feature picture had begun.

The sudden squeal of tires stopped Allie's heart. Visions of what happened earlier; the car jumping the curb and heading straight for her nearly made her pee her pants.

On the huge screen before her, a police chase was in progress. The cruiser chased the Thunderbird through intersections, around corners at speeds that chilled her to the bone.

The knowledge it was only the movie, not an actual dark sedan careening toward her, wasn't enough to chase the tremors that shook her to the very core of her existence.

Allie felt powerless to stop the fear gripping her. The walls began to close in on her. She literally felt like something crawled beneath her skin. She hadn't realized it, but her fingernails were now embedded into Jake's arm as she clung to him. Only his long sleeve denim shirt protected his skin. He pressed his jeans-clad thigh close to hers as if trying to reassure her all was okay.

She heard Jake's breath of relief when she released him.

Allie tugged at her light blue sweater. "Jake. Let's get out of here." She didn't wait for his response, she was already on her feet moving quickly down the steps.

Even though she knew the echo of footsteps behind her were Jake's, fear washed over her in a sudden wave that threatened to pull her into its inky depths.

Her throat tightened. She felt a tingling in her hands, feet and lips as she gasped for air. The picture on the screen skewed, blurring to make her lightheaded, dizzy.

Panic followed swiftly. She missed the next step and began to fall.

Fleeting snapshots appeared and vanished in her mind. Running. Crying. Shouts and screams. Swirling water—always the raging river as she fell.

Strong hands gripped her from behind. A frantic whimper squeezed from her lungs. Once again, she was in the jungle—running for her life.

Desperately, she flailed her arms, fighting her attacker. "No," she screamed as lights flashed in the darkness. The roar in her head continued to elevate, drowning her cries. Her struggle was promptly subdued as powerful arms pulled her into an ironclad embrace. She couldn't move held so tightly to a rock-hard chest.

"Allie. Stop," Jake whispered firmly. His cheek pressed against hers. "It's me. Jake."

"Jake?" Oh God. What had just happened to her?

Every bone in Allie's body melted, softening so that she felt like the only thing holding her upright was Jake's grasp. Her heart was racing, pounding against her chest.

"Breathe slower," Jake encouraged. "You're hyperventilating."

It took a moment to slow her short, rapid pants, even longer for her surroundings to materialize.

She was in a movie theater—not the jungles of Peru.

Jake held her—not her enemy.

From the corner of her eye, she could see the curious stares pointed in their direction. God, she'd made such a fool of herself. She buried her head against Jake's shoulder, fighting tears she refused to shed. Still she couldn't stop the uncontrollable shaking.

Jake drew her nearer. "It's okay, honey."

A movie attendant beamed his flashlight on them, turning their attention to him. "Is everything okay?" The tall, slender boy of about seventeen gaped at them with concern. "Does she need medical assistance?"

"No. She's fine." Arm now around her shoulders, Jake escorted Allie past the attendant, down the remaining stairs, through the lobby, and out the glass doors. They didn't stop until they were several feet away from the swarm of people buying tickets outside.

Night had fallen. The stars in the heavens were barely visible as clouds began to erase them from the sky. The smoke from the pit barbeque restaurant next door filled her lungs. In the distance the sounds of the freeway could be heard, as well as the soft music provided by the theater. Several noisy toddlers ran past Allie and Jake, jerking them to a halt to avoid running over them. Two flustered parents increased their steps to catch up with their children.

Through dull eyes, Allie gazed up at Jake. "I'm so sorry."

His brief smile was so tender. "Nothing to be sorry about." He held her close as if he were shielding her from the crowd with his own body. He scanned the parking lot quickly before moving toward his truck.

How could she have been so stupid? Her attempts to prove she wasn't frightened, that she wouldn't allow whoever was terrorizing her to win, had failed miserably.

She was scared—scared shitless.

But more important, Allie realized that Jake's life could be in jeopardy, too. What if her assailant shot at her again and missed hitting Jake or one of the small children who just passed by?

The thought made Allie sick. She swallowed hard, attempting to force the guilt crawling up her throat back down.

The sour taste made her insides churn, hot tears beat at the back of her eyelids. She wouldn't cry. She was through crying.

"Jake, let's go home."

There was no need to ask twice. His stride was quick, leading her through the parking lot, past one vehicle and then the next, until they reached his truck. Without pausing, he activated the locks, held open the passenger door, and she crawled in. He moved quickly around the truck and got in, securing the locks immediately before starting the engine. All the while, he didn't once stop taking in their surroundings. Alert, he appeared ready for anything.

No one spoke on the ride back home. She nibbled at the loose cuticle hanging on her thumb, biting until she left the area raw. Unconsciously, she started on a different area.

Jake glanced over at her. "Stop that, Allie."

She released a heavy sigh dropping her hand into her lap only to have her fingers start picking at the area she'd last bitten.

What had she done to infuriate someone to want her dead? Was it someone from Brayer Tech? A scientist? What happen in Peru? Why couldn't she remember? Or was it someone else? Someone from her past?

"You okay?" Jake asked, steering the truck into the driveway. The garage door made a moaning sound as it rose and they disappeared inside.

She flashed him a *you're-kidding-right?* look.

He flinched.

Dammit. This isn't his fault. She wouldn't be alive it hadn't been for Jake pulling her out of the way of the vehicle this morning.

She fought the irritation crawling across her skin that turned to another unhealthy dose of guilt. "Sorry. I'm just so—" the word stuck in her throat before it burst free, "—mad." An angry tear rolled down her cheek. "Fuck." The single word held all the frustration she felt bubbling up inside her ready to burst free.

He opened his door and got out. Before he reached Allie's door, she was already swinging it open.

"I'm not to blame for what happen in Peru. I didn't destroy their research. I-I'm leaving."

"What?" There was no way in hell Jake was letting her out of his sight.

She stood before him, her backbone rigid, her chin slightly raised in determination. "I've decided to leave town tomorrow."

Without realizing what he was doing, he grasped her by the arms and gave her a little shake. "The hell you are. You'll keep your ass right here where I can watch over you." Just the thought of losing her again made him sick inside.

He couldn't—wouldn't let her go.

She batted her eyelashes, chasing away the moisture that began to pool in her eyes. Something akin to pain tightened her face. "Watch over me? And who is supposed to watch over you?"

Her words caught him completely off guard. "Me?"

She walloped him on the chest with both fists. "Yeah. You." Tears swelled, but didn't fall. "I couldn't live if something happened to you." She licked her lips nervously.

Jake harrumphed away her concern as tender emotion sent goose bumps across his arms.

She cared.

Maybe not like he wanted her too, but she did care.

"Ahhh...honey." He pulled her trembling body into his embrace. "Nothing is going to happen to me."

She wrapped her arms around his waist and buried her head against his chest. "You don't know that."

He had been so preoccupied with Allie's safety, he hadn't even thought of his own. She was right, but it didn't change the fact she wasn't leaving, not now—not ever.

"Jake, I'm leaving," she mumbled, but even as she spoke, her grip tightened around him.

Finger beneath her chin, he raised her gaze to meet his. He looked her directly in the eyes. "No, you're not."

She frowned, narrowing her gaze on him. "Yes, I am."

"No," he repeated more firmly.

Anger heated her face. "You pigheaded man. I'll leave if I want to." Palms against his chest, she pushed hard. He grabbed her wrists. Clenching her jaw, she released a growl of frustration.

Jake's cock stirred beneath her hot glare. There was nothing like Alison Grant enraged. She was magnificent. Her chest rose, her beautiful nipples pressing against the black sweater she wore. The tendons in her neck tightened.

He gave her another shake, as if he could rattle some sense into her. "You'll stay here, so I can keep you safe."

The expression on her face screamed *out-of-my-way*. He should have known no matter what he said when Allie's mind was made up there wasn't any way to dissuade her.

She stomped her foot, barely missing his. "The hell I will—"

He stole her words away with a demanding kiss. There was no tenderness in his touch. He took what he wanted, spearing his fingers through her hair to grasp the nape of her neck and pulled her deeper into his caress.

She tasted of fire and ice. Her resistance was countered by the ardent stroke of her tongue against his as if they battled for supremacy.

In this domain—he was alpha.

And he would love her so thoroughly, when tonight was over she would never think of leaving town or him.

The fervent cry she released when their lips parted warmed his blood to a boiling point. He shoved his hands beneath her sweater, pushing past her bra to cup her heavy breasts. Her nipples were rigid peaks between his fingers. With no mercy, he rolled, pinched and tugged at them.

"Release me," she fumed. Desire simmered in the depths of her eyes.

Instead of appeasing her, he bent and took one of her bare nipples into his mouth and bit.

She threw back her head and screamed a high-pitched wail somewhere between pain and pleasure. Hands fisted, she pulled his hair, a sweet ache that made him suck even harder, pausing only to drag his teeth across the sensitive skin.

Arching into him, she groaned, "Dammit, Jake. I've got to leave." There was a whine in her voice that said she really didn't want to go.

His mouth made a pop when he released her nipple and he stood to meet her eye to eye. "Allie, you won't ever leave me." With one hand, he grabbed her wrists and drew them above her head, while his other arm snaked around her back to hold her close.

Her brows shot up. "Oh and why not?"

"Because after tonight you'll never want to leave." He dipped a finger beneath the waistband of her jeans into the crease of her ass. "The things I'll do to you, you've only dreamed about."

Interest sparked in her eyes, but not her facial features. "You're pretty high on yourself. You'll need something better than that to make me stay."

"Then try this one on for size. I love you—always have. And I'll never let you go."

God, did he really say that aloud? He was a bigger fool than he thought.

Mouth open, eyes astonished, all she could do was stare at him as he stepped away from her and walked into the house.

Chapter Seventeen

I love you—always have.

Jake's admission wrapped around Allie's heart and squeezed, leaving her breathless. Like a statue, she froze to watch Jake disappear from the garage into the house. She stared at the door long after he'd gone, wondering if she had only imagined his declaration of love. Cool air stroked her exposed breasts, her bra and black sweater hiked up where Jake had pushed them.

"How dare you," she huffed, stuffing her breasts back into her bra and yanking down her sweater. She crammed her hands into her jeans pockets, because she didn't know what else to do with them.

He spoke words of love and then walked away. Talk about leaving a girl hanging on a ledge.

But the truth was Allie couldn't fight the excitement and thrill she felt stirring inside her. She struggled to sort out her thoughts and feelings, but everything felt magnified. Her body was numb, but strangely alive. The tingle from his fiery kiss remained upon her lips. His absent touch made her breasts ache for more. Her arms felt empty.

Not to mention, the ticking of the clock on the garage wall seemed to echo in her ears. The chill in the air made her feel bare, stripped of her defenses. Her light sweater did nothing to chase the cold away. The scent of gas and oil permeated the air, but not above the masculine scent that lingered and held his image in her mind.

What was real and what was just smoke and mirrors?

Did she share Jake's feelings or was the giddiness she felt each time he entered a room a bad case of lust? Was it the predicament she was facing or something shallower, a need to hold onto her memories through him?

Jake and the house were all Allie had left in the entire world.

Yet when she realized that Jake could be in danger, she was willing to give both him and the house up to ensure his safety.

Didn't she get points for that?

The truth was she didn't want to leave. More honestly, she didn't want to leave Jake.

When had he become so important to her? The idea that she had allowed the man to slip beneath her skin aroused and angered her. Little by little, he had taken control. House. Memories. Now her heart.

Yes. Her heart.

Jake told her he loved her and disappeared.

She jerked her hands out of her pockets. Her fingers curled into fists. "Damn you for dropping a bomb like that and then just leaving." She stomped toward the door, jerked it open. The house was quiet. Several lights illuminated her way as she moved swiftly through the dining room to the living room and up the stairs.

She burst into Jake's bedroom, planting her hands on her hips. "You can't say something like that and—"

He was naked, propped into a sitting position on the bed. One arm draped over a bent knee. Arching proudly against his abdomen, his firm erection jutted from the patch of dark hair between his thighs.

Dark and sensuous, he gazed up and down her length, making her feel as if he peeled away her clothing one at a time.

He looked so damn sexy. She gasped, air caught somewhere between her lungs and her mouth. She managed to finish her sentence. "—and just walk away."

Curling a finger, he beckoned her to his side.

"Jake." Anxiety made his name come out a squeak. She cleared her throat, before she swiped her tongue across her lips. "We need to talk."

He shook his head. A wisp of ebony hair fell over one eye. The small action increased the heat building in her body. Heavy breasts and aching nipples joined the moisture growing between her thighs.

She shifted her feet, not remembering the last time she felt so unsure of herself. "Did you mean what you said?"

Flashing a drop-dead sexy smile, he curled his finger again. "Come here and let me show you just how much."

His cock twitched, drawing her attention. He was so long and thick, so male. Heat spread across her cheeks. She jerked her eyes back to his. "Uh…I think we should talk."

He raised a haughty brow. "I think we should make love."

Unexpectedly, she burst into laughter. "Damn you, Jake. You're trying to rattle me."

He patted the bed beside him. "No. I'm trying to get you into my bed."

She fought the smile tugging at the corners of her mouth. "Well, that too." Allie stroked him with her gaze. From his head to his toes, he was perfection. Spread out on his velour comforter he looked good enough to eat. And Lord knew she wanted to join him.

Focus. Take your mind out of the gutter where it's heading and focus.

"You just can't drop something like I l-lo—" She couldn't quite get the words out. "Say those three words and then leave."

Tight, controlled movements moved him to his knees. Sleek and wild, he looked predacious, stalking his prey, as his hands touched the bed and he crawled toward her.

"Would you rather hear that I've loved you since high school? Or that I see your face in every woman I meet?" He slipped off the bed and moved to stand before her. "Maybe it would make a difference if I told you the four years you've been gone have been hell? Do you have any idea how long I've waited to hold you in my arms?"

He didn't pause for her to answer. Instead, he held his arms open and she walked willingly into them.

With a finger, he brushed back a lock of her hair. "Dammit, Allie. I love you. I always have." He sealed his affirmation with a kiss to leave no doubt he spoke the truth.

It was tender, almost heartbreaking, as his lips moved over hers. She opened to him, driving her tongue forward to tangle with his. He sipped from her mouth, drank as if she offered him the elixir of life.

And he held her, gently, like she might break. His touch was light, caressing, everything a woman could ask for.

Cherish.

Adore.

Love.

Those were only a few words that came to mind, effectively breaking her resistance and pulling her into his world.

She smoothed her hands down his chest, his waist, to pause a moment at his hip. She moved lower to cup the weight of his balls with one hand.

So hard, yet so soft.

Allie gave herself up to the feel and taste of him as they continued to kiss. Between two fingers, she stretched the loose skin of his scrotum, moving and fondling his testicles back and forth. He scooted his feet further apart, giving her more access. As her fingers folded around his cock, he sucked in a ragged breath, parting their lips.

Their gazes met in a fiery exchange.

His nostrils flared, almost as if he scented her. The look in his eyes was primitive, hungry.

He didn't have to ask. She knew what he wanted.

Bringing both hands up to his neck, she curled her fingers and dragged her nails downward, leaving soft red marks in their path. She scraped them across his taut nipples and he moaned from the pleasure.

His heated expression got hotter, adding to her arousal. Her nipples rasped against her bra. A tightening pinched low in her belly.

Her gaze pinned to his, she lowered her mouth and swirled her tongue around each hard nipple, before continuing onward.

His bellybutton also received a little tongue action.

Evidently, he had waited long enough, because he placed his palms on her shoulders and pushed her to her knees.

"Now," was all he said, and even that came out strangled, a harsh whisper.

A bead of pre-come glistened on the crown of his erection jutting before her. She took him into her hand, excitement releasing between her thighs. Slowly, she leaned forward and lapped the pearl away. A shudder rippled through him.

He fisted her hair and thrust his hips forward against her lips.

She gave him a half-smile before she took him deep into her mouth.

"Fuck." Another tremor shook him. His hips matched the glide of her lips.

Her tongue smoothed up and down his length, feeling the bulging vein that ran through it. She brought her teeth into play, scraping gently down the side of his cock.

He released a suppressed groan and tried to pull her away, but she drew him deep, sucking harder. She knew the moment he surrendered. The hold he had on her hair tightened, he pulled her closer. The movement of his hips sped up. He pumped in and out of her mouth, driving to the back of throat, until a cry tore from him. His body tensed for an instant and then he shattered.

Come jetted to the back of her throat, warm and salty. She swallowed, again and again, each movement wringing out another cry of ecstasy from him.

"Stop," Jake half-moaned, half-laughed. "You're killing me." But what a fucking way to go. He was so sensitive that even the touch of her tongue against his dying erection made him shiver and shake. When she released him, he assisted her to her feet.

Seductively, her eyes closed. "Mmmm..." The tip of her tongue traced her lips as if relishing his taste. Her eyelids rose. A devilish smile on her face.

He slid his hand behind the nape of her neck and jerked her closer. Their lips inches away.

She laughed. Her eyes sparkled with merriment.

He gave her a little shake. "I'm in the mind to punish you for teasing me like that."

"I don't know what you're talking about." She feigned innocence.

He pressed his body against hers. "Uhhh…lying. That earns you another punishment."

She batted her lashes. "Oh, my. What will you do to me?" The gleam in her eyes said she was ready to play.

Jake went to his treasure chest of toys and found a length of rope and a silk scarf. "Follow me," he said, leading the way toward the hanging plants in the corner. He removed one and then began to wrap the silk scarf around her wrists. He looped that material through the chain, then went to the wall to adjust the length. He pulled the chain tight, so that her arms were drawn above her head, and affixed it to the wall.

"Uh…did you forget something?"

"Not a thing," he assured.

She smirked, tossing her hair behind her. "I'm still dressed."

"I know." He flashed a smirk of his own. "Spread your legs about five inches apart," he ordered.

A frown chased her mirth away, but she did as he asked. A silky sensation slithered across her skin as he tied the rope around her knees.

Jake stood behind her, her sweater soft against his skin, as he reached around to grasp her breasts.

"Do you know what happens when you're aroused?" She remained silent, her head bowed, watching as he began to draw large circles around her breasts, reducing the size of the circles with each rotation. "Your temperature rises." He plucked at her hardened nubs through her sweater, then flattened out his palms and smoothed his hands over her tips. "As your body heat rises you have the uncontrollable urge to strip, but in this case you won't be able to."

Allie raised her head. "I don't think I like this game." Already her chest rose and fell faster than just minutes ago.

"It's a punishment. You're not supposed to." He pushed his hand between her jeans-clad thighs and began a slow friction, pressing against where he knew her sensitive clit hid.

Whether it was a reaction or intentional, she laid her head back upon his shoulder and started to ride his hand, moving her hips back and forth in rhythm with his movements. He felt the moment she tried to widen her legs, but the binding around her knees held her steady.

Her arousal had already soaked through her panties and jeans. "You're wet." He stated the obvious, continuing to stroke her, as his other hand began plucking at a nipple once again.

When Allie tensed, he lightened his touch, bringing her back down. As her breathing leveled out, he started all over again.

She growled in frustration each time.

The problem with this form of punishment was that he shared in it. He wanted her naked. His rock-hard cock throbbed against her ass. Just the thought of her legs parted so he could delve between them and taste her nectar was driving him crazy. He wanted to hear her scream his name. So when she said, "Please?" he gave in, releasing the bindings around her wrists and knees.

That was not much fun at all.

Liar.

As Jake had predicted, Allie's body temperature hit a new high. She ached to be touched. Her clothes hugged her as if they were two sizes too small, suffocating, she needed to get out of them.

Immediately, she started to rip her sweater off. Jake stopped her with a hand to hers. "This is for my pleasure. I'll undress you."

Jake knelt before her, removing each of her tennis shoes and then her socks. His fingers moved swiftly to undo the button and zipper of her jeans. Warm hands skimmed along her skin, pulling her pants down her legs. It felt awkward to be fully dressed from the waist up and bare-assed. She didn't have to wait long before she stood just as naked as Jake.

"On the bed." He moved toward his box of goodies and pulled out the large dildo.

She almost choked, stopping in her footsteps. "Uh...isn't that used for a prank?"

"No," he said frankly, gathering a few other things.

"Well, I'm not sure that will fit any of my orifices."

He burst out in laughter and set the dildo back down. "Actually, I just wanted to see your reaction." Turnabout was fair play. She had teased him, now it was his turn. "In reality a woman's body is made to accommodate something this large." He winked at her. "With a little time and patience anything is possible."

"Haha." In all honesty, she breathed a sigh of relief.

That thing was huge.

"I have something else in mind for you." He opened his palm and inside was a small silver bullet. Attached to it by a long cord was a controller.

Now that looked like fun.

Anxiously, she crawled upon the bed and waited. They needed to talk, but not now.

He set the controller, a tube of lubricant, a wet wipe and two condoms on the side of the bed and joined her. Both in a kneeling position, their bodies came together. He pressed his lips to hers, before he whispered, "I'm going to fuck you hard. Grab the headboard and hold on." A wicked smile curved his lips.

Allie's nipples drew impossibly harder, the tingle driving her wild as she slid to her back and grasped the railing above her head. Automatically, her legs opened wide.

She was ready—more than ready.

The tightening low her belly made her circle her hips, trying to appease the pang, but it did no good. She needed Jake inside her to ease the throbbing.

The damn man knew it too. He took his sweet time to climb on the bed. Slow and easy, he crawled between her thighs, kneeling, as he smoothed his palms down her chests, over her breasts, until he cradled them in his hands.

"Please, Jake. Fuck me now."

Jake chuckled. "First things first." He reached for a condom, tore open the package, and sheathed himself. The other condom he placed over the silver bullet and lavished it with lubricant.

No secret where that toy was going.

Allie's rosebud puckered.

The gel was cool sliding across her tight entrance as he began to prepare her. When his finger slipped inside, she gasped. The burn lasted only a second before his finger pumping in and out made her push against his hand, wanting more. Instead, he pulled from her and used the wet wipe to cleanse his hands.

"Ready?" he teased her.

"Jake!" Allie was about to explode. "Please."

A breath lodged in her lungs as she felt the nudge against her ass. He pushed and her body swallowed up the small toy.

"Ahhh..." she sighed, relishing the foreign object stretching her tight.

A turn of the dial and vibrator came alive.

Allie screamed out and jerked so hard he had to tighten his hold on her hips. She had never felt anything like it before. White-hot fingers of sensation shot up her rectum, igniting every nerve. She tried to arch, ease the pleasure-pain, but Jake held her firmly in place.

"Oh, my God," she choked, seeing the flush on her face in the mirror above. "Jake, I'm going to come."

She had never reached this height of arousal so quickly. It was as if the vibrator pushed the right button inside her or maybe it was the foreplay. Either way Allie knew there was no way she could hold on.

Before she could inhale, he had released her. His strong frame pressed atop her smaller one, widening her thighs in the process. With one thrust, he buried his cock deep, filling her with the most incredible fullness.

He rocked against her, his hot gaze pinned on hers. "Come for me, Allie." She didn't need his encouragement.

Every fiber in her snapped at once.

Her back came off the bed. She screamed a throaty cry of rapture.

Her climax shattered with a force that felt like voltage surging through her body, burning everything in its path. As she writhed uncontrollably beneath Jake, she heard him moan, join her. While he remained rigid, his orgasm tearing through him, she couldn't stop moving. Her entire body was afire.

Moisture wept from the corner of her eyes.

The throb threatened to never end.

Soon the vibration inside her anus subsided. The pulse in her pussy began slowly dying. She gulped a mouthful of air and then another. Her heart palpitated, beating against her chest. Her skin felt clammy. She was shaking. She fought to swallow the lump in her throat.

As she lay upon the bed boneless, she felt Jake extract the silver bullet. Within seconds, a warm wet washcloth smoothed across her now tender genitals.

The bed groaned beneath Jake's weight as he crawled upon it. "Leaving me?"

She turned her head and looked at him through half-shuttered eyes. "Never." Then her eyelids fell and she drifted asleep.

Chapter Eighteen

Angry black clouds stole what was left of day. The storm that had been building for several days had arrived.

Just Allie's luck.

She stared into the darkness for a moment longer, before releasing the drape and letting it swing shut. As she turned away, a sudden crack of thunder made her jump. Her skin prickled, teasing the hair on her arms.

This was not how she'd planned her night of seduction. Disappointed, she looked around the bedroom. The scene was set with a dozen candles burning softly. Their sweet and aromatic scent gave the room a warm, sensuous feel. Fuzzy red handcuffs replaced the hanging plants that dangled from the chains in the corner. Earlier she had rolled up the rug, baring the D-rings on the floor.

"Yeah. You thought of everything, but the weather," she grumbled, looking at the little silver bullet she had laid out upon the bed. Last night had been earth-shattering.

A sudden chill skittering across her exposed skin robbed her of the excitement she had experienced when she slipped on the skin-tight, black leather corset Jake had bought her. She had felt downright wicked decked out in the matching thong, fishnet stockings, fingerless gloves, and stilettos.

Now she was worried and cold. The chill of the evening danced across her bare skin. Being half naked did that to a girl.

She glanced at the clock on the wall. Six-thirty.

Jake was late.

The sharp heels of her stilettos clicked across the floor as she went to the drawer and extracted Jake's robe. Slipping her arms into the sleeves, the soft material swallowed her up, hanging past her fingertips. She pushed the sleeves up, but they fell back down. She was fiddling with the sleeves, trying to roll them up, when a spine-tingling screech jerked her around.

The flutter in her chest tightened, rooting her to the floor.

The long, drawn-out rasp sounded again. An uneasy chuckle pushed from her thin lips. It was only the wind dragging a branch of the large maple tree against the window.

A breath of relief approached on swift feet. Yet Allie couldn't chase away the jittery sensation that made her heart pound, her pulse race.

Agitated, she paced the room and then headed for the open door. "Jake, where are you?"

Maybe the weather had delayed him or he had a problem on the job site. The excuses were meant to soothe her, but they didn't. The thought of him possibly being hurt or worse made her shudder.

"You're being silly."

As she descended the stairs, she remembered her faceless tormentor still walked the streets—waiting to strike again.

"Jeez, Allie." She released a huff of reprimand. "Jake's only thirty minutes late. A little weather and you lose it."

On the last step, her heel caught the hem of the robe and she stumbled into the living room barely finding her footing. Frustrated, she yanked the robe together, tying the sash.

A small fire burned in the hearth, its heat barely noticeable. She sat in her mother's recliner, pulled her legs beneath her, watching the flickering flames pop and dance about, ignoring the television that she'd left on earlier.

When did Jake start meaning so much to her?

A soft sigh made her smile. Last night had been amazing, erasing for the moment the fact that someone wanted her dead.

Jake loved her. He didn't want her to leave and she didn't want to go.

She shook her head. Damned if she hadn't fallen for him too. Who knew if it was love? But it was becoming harder and harder to get the man out of her head.

The hollow rat-a-tat against the chimney announced that it had started to rain. Instead of getting up and stoking the fire, she wrapped her arms around herself.

That's when the ceiling light flickered off and on.

Dread twisted her gut. Allie's heart skipped a beat. Slowly, she drew her feet from beneath her and set them on the floor.

"Please," she prayed aloud, "don't go out." She stared hard at the lights as if she could will electricity. Another flicker and a sharp pop, the lights blinked out.

Frozen, a strangled whimper squeezed from her tight lips. The fireplace gave off some light, but not enough to comfort her. Allie strained to hear movement, signs that she was alone.

Of course, she was being paranoid. These things happen in a storm. Lights went out. Wind tossed branches around, making it sound like fingernails against a chalkboard. Boyfriends were late getting home.

And if every horror movie she had seen was true, crimes—especially murder—were committed on nights just like this one.

Allie tried to laugh the ridiculous thought away, but a crash of thunder forced a tight cry from her. A torrent of rain pelted the windows, as the heavens opened up and released their fury.

The sudden ring of the telephone made Allie jump to her feet. Scrambling for the receiver, she moved so quickly that she knocked the telephone off the table to the floor. Her hands were shaking by the time she pressed the telephone to her ear.

"Allie?" Through the crackling of his cell phone, she could hear Jake's concern.

She clenched the receiver. "Jake, where are you?"

"Is everything okay?"

"Yeah. The electricity went out. I dropped the phone." She tried to hide the tremor that shook her. Just hearing his voice gave her some comfort.

"Honey, I have to meet with a new customer. The restaurant he chose is just down the road from the job site. Will you be okay for a while longer?"

Disappointment weighed heavily. She took a calming breath before she lied. "Don't be silly. Of course I'll be okay."

"I won't be long," he promised. "Love you."

She grinned and opened her mouth to respond when the phone disconnected.

Allie's smile faded. Now that her eyes had adjusted to the darkness, she gathered the telephone off the floor and placed the receiver in its cradle.

Surprised, but pleased when the lights flickered back on, she said, "Thank you, God." Her shoulders fell with a deep sigh of relief.

The heater kicked on, making a humming noise, followed by the refrigerator and television. She started to ease back into the chair when knocking on the door made her pause.

"Who could that be?" She stood staring at the door, only moving to answer it when the rapping started anew. She closed her fingers around the doorknob, and then she jerked her hand away releasing it. Instead of opening the door, she pressed her eye to the peephole.

A shadowy figure stood just beyond the door.

Anxiety slithered across Allie's arms. She started to back away just as lightning cracked, illuminating the man's face.

"Tom." He was back from Bulgaria and standing on her porch. Rain beat down in sheets, as she quickly gained her composure, unlocked the door and flung it wide. "Tom."

She remembered the beautiful grin that met her, but it did nothing to her—not as it had when they first met. Short blond hair, good looks, and roguish smirk, he could captivate a woman. He had definitely charmed her.

"Allie." He took her in his arms, hugging her tightly to his wet body.

"You're soaking wet." She withdrew, wiggling out of his embrace. "Get in here."

As he stepped inside, water ran off his overcoat to pool at his feet. With a sheepish half grin, he said, "Sorry."

"It's okay. Let me get some towels." She started moving toward the kitchen.

When she returned, Tom's coat was draped in the bend of his arm. His hair was plastered to his head. She took his coat, handed him a towel, and dropped a couple on the floor. As he towel-dried his hair, she mopped up the floor, scooting the towels beneath his coat now hanging on the coat rack.

After swiping the towel across his face, Tom held it out to her. As she reached for it, he jerked her into his arms.

"Baby, I've missed you so much." His warm breath washed over her face. He nibbled lightly on her neck.

Allie couldn't breathe.

The woody fragrance of sandalwood slammed into her. A scent she had once enjoyed, but now made her a bit queasy. Perhaps he wore too much. Maybe she felt uncomfortable held by a man she had no feelings for. The truth was she had been looking forward to Jake's embrace all day long. Seeing Tom again was something she hadn't expected.

Guilt. Yeah. That had to be it.

Whatever it was, she found herself discreetly shrugging out of his arms once again.

His smile faltered. "You okay?"

Towel in her hands, she turned away, refusing to met his gaze. "Sure. Of course. Everything is fine."

A chill raced up her back as strong hands on her shoulders turned her around.

A shadow glimmered in his eyes, but faded as fast as it appeared. With a gentle touch, he smoothed his knuckles along her jawline. "What's up, baby?" His husky voice stroked her as keenly as the palm he trailed down her neck. The light squeeze he gave her made her windpipe clamp shut.

Panic. Sharp and raw, it widened her eyes and forced a gasp from her parted lips. Heavy-lidded, he leaned into her for a kiss. Before he could press his mouth to hers, she pushed him away leaving him standing there, stunned.

"God, I'm sorry." She covered her mouth with her palm. She fought to breathe, putting distance between them.

What the hell is wrong with me?

Allie was jittery in a way that surprised her. This was Tom—an ex-lover.

Suspicion rimmed his eyes. His jaws clenched. "We've always been honest with each other. What's going on?" There was a hard edge to his question.

She hated the fact that he had come all this way to see her. "Dammit. Tom, I wish you had called." There wasn't any easy way to say it, and she wasn't one to beat around the bush. "There's someone else."

For a moment, he looked almost relieved. "I see." He approached to stand before her once again. "No chance in rekindling what we had?"

God, this was hard.

She shook her head. What was even more difficult was admitting that she was indeed in love with Jake. The man had snagged her, hook, line, and sinker. She fought to hide the smile that wanted to burst free.

Tom's shoulders fell with resignation. "I guess I'd better leave." Silently, he turned, but she stopped him with a hand upon his arm.

"No please." There were so many unanswered questions. She had hoped he could shed some light. "Tom, about that night…what happened?"

ꕤ

Applebee's was packed. The sports bar was filled with an array of people, families, couples, and beered-up basketball fans. Only thirty minutes remained of happy hour and the servers were a swarm of bees buzzing around, taking and delivering drink orders and food. The sweet scent of barbeque sauce caressed Jake's nose as a waiter passed by with a plate of ribs.

Jake took a swig of his beer and checked the clock on his cell phone. Thomas King was supposed to have arrived thirty minutes ago. As the Arizona State University's Sun Devils made a three-point basket, a group of men sprang to their feet cheering.

Through the darkened windows, Jake could see the rain had increased. It struck the windows like BB's making pinging sounds. He wondered if the weather had delayed King. But most of all he worried about Allie. She didn't sound convincing that all was okay.

He checked the time once again.

King's job included a subdivision of twenty-five houses, which meant that Jake would need to hire more employees. Money was tight, but with a large advance, he should be able to swing it.

Oh, who was he kidding?

He'd do anything for this job. Jake had even changed out of his coveralls to a new corduroy sports jacket, shirt and jeans. And he didn't do that for just anyone.

"Another one?" a dark-brunette in tight blue jeans asked, as she raked her interested gaze over him.

Jake quickly emptied his glass and handed it to her. "Yeah. One more." One more and then if King didn't arrive he was going home. It was cold and damp. Jake knew a woman who was warm, willing and waiting for him.

Chapter Nineteen

Sitting next to Tom on the couch, Allie wrung her hands, unaware that her robe had fallen open and her fishnet stockings as well as a good portion of her leg and thigh was visible. That was until she saw the gleam of appreciation in Tom's eyes. He raised a brow and grinned. She yanked the robe closed, feeling the heat of embarrassment across her face.

An awkward silence lingered between them.

"How much do you remember about that night?" Tom's gaze scanned her body until he met her eyes.

"Very little." She hated talking about that night—hated feeling so victimized. But she was at the point she'd do anything to remember. "I get flashes of memory—or more like nightmares."

Tom leaned back. Yet there was something odd about how uncomfortable, stiff, his body appeared. "About what?"

The breath Allie released came out shaky, a small broken gasp of air. "The jungle." She stared into her lap, clutching her hands. It was hard enough waking to this night after night. Now she had to relive it with Tom.

"Damp air." As she began to speak, everything about that night rose violently to the surface. Sights, sounds, and smells so real they made her pause to steady herself. "Decay—rotting vegetation. Smoke. Fire. Screams." She glanced up at Tom. He stared at her intently. "And running. Someone chasing me."

He sat up straight, moved closer. "Who? It was a madhouse that night. Maybe it was just someone trying to escape the fire. There were people running all over the place. Not only were the huts ablaze, but parts of the forest. I tried to find you."

"No." She placed a hand on his thigh. "Tom, I must have seen something that night. Someone is trying to kill me."

Tom's disbelief came out in the form of laughter. He patted her hand. "Alison, you're being silly."

"Silly." Her voice screeched. She touched the bullet wound on her head. "I've been shot at and nearly run over by a car." Her pulse sped. Anger helped to keep her in control. "I'm getting crank calls."

He regarded her with an expression of concern. "This is inconceivable. What do the police say?"

"No leads. My safety is in my own hands."

His fingertips caressed her cheek. His touch was unwelcome. "And the doctors? Will you ever get your memory back?"

Allie shrugged. "It may or may not return."

"What do you think?"

She squared her shoulders. "I will remember. And when I do, I'll nail the sonofabitch's ass to the wall."

Tom laughed again, but this time his amusement sounded a little strained. "Okay. So what else do you remember?"

A shiver shook her. "Cruel hands grabbing me from behind, trapping me against his body. The strong scent of sandalwood." Allie's eyes widened with surprise. She jerked her gaze to Tom. He wore sandalwood cologne.

She had never been able to give a name to the scent that haunted her—her attacker's essence. It surrounded her as he held her close and whispered against her ear that he hadn't wanted to hurt her. That he had actually grown fond of her.

Like a dam bursting, sparks of memory chased one after another.

The fire blazing.

Gray smoke funneling into the sky.

Her screams joining the ones in the distance.

Desperately, she ran further and further away from the campsite. Pain and fear escalated as he caught her and began to drag her through the jungle by one arm.

Sounds of the waterfall growing louder and louder.

A cliff.

Raging waters below.

Jerked around to face her attacker. The push—the fall over the edge.

Allie gasped.

It was all so clear.

Tom's face.

His cruel touch.

Heart pounding, mouth dry with fear, Allie lurched off the couch. With a cry, she broke into a run. She stumbled on the first step. Missing the banister, she went down hard upon her knees. Pain splintered. She floundered for only a breath, before crawling, trying to get to her feet.

Cold fingers closed around her ankle.

She screamed.

"It was only a matter of time before you remembered." His ominous tone chilled her.

Twisting and turning, a wild kick struck him against the cheek.

"Fuck." His fingers slipped from her ankle. He blinked, grabbing thin air, before curling his fingers into her robe.

Frantically, Allie yanked her arms free of the robe. Her heels made getting to her feet difficult. Half-running, half-crawling, she glanced over her shoulder. Light glistened off of something in his hand.

Knife.

A stitch caught in her side. Another scream froze in her throat.

At the top of the stairs, she darted toward Jake's bedroom. She ran inside, slammed the door closed, but not before it came to a stop.

"Allie, don't make this harder than it has to be. I would have never hurt you if you hadn't discovered me."

"Bullshit." Allie couldn't think. Memories bombarded her. She had fallen asleep at her computer. A noise woke her, Tom riffling through her files. The smell of kerosene. He hadn't answered her when she asked what he was doing. Instead he attacked.

Allie threw her weight against the door.

Too late.

The door swung wide, flinging her against the wall. Her head hit with a bang. Stars burst behind her eyelids. Her ears rang. She slithered to the floor.

When the daze cleared, Tom stood over her.

There was something wrong with him. Something terribly wrong.

A wild expression burned in his eyes. She recognized the same glow on that horrible night her life changed forever.

He smiled. Not the roguish smile she had found so charming, but one hard, edged with cruelty. The same sadistic smirk as he pushed her over the waterfall.

Allie remembered it all.

Keyboard to the head, he had knocked her out cold. After she had awakened, the hut was ablaze.

Tom had left her there to die.

She choked on the next memory. Smoke so thick, she had barely found the window to wiggle out of before the roof collapsed. Her throat burned. She coughed, sucking in clean breaths of air.

Tom's surprise when he saw her as he was exiting another hut that burst into flames.

Allie recalled running—running for her life.

"So it's all coming back." It wasn't a question. Somehow he knew she was reliving that night.

She gasped again, feeling a thick, moist layer of fog surround her. The same that threatened to swallow her up as she fell over a knotted liana root worming across the ground. It was hard to breathe. The heart-wrenching screams of the villagers echoed in her ears.

Not real. She inhaled, trying to find something to anchor her.

"Why?" was all she managed to ask.

"Why?" His lips curled, his face contorting into a snarl. "Brayer Tech." Hatred she had never before witnessed hung on those two words. A red mottled look of fury raced up his neck, exploding across cheeks. "The scientists were about to announce a breakthrough cure for Alzheimer's, a medicine that would prevent the deterioration of the part of the brain that causes the disease. I couldn't let that happen."

"I don't understand." Even as she spoke, visions of her struggle with Tom on the edge of the cliff penetrated her mind. A roar began in her head, the same deafening roar of the waterfall as they moved closer to the edge. Whitecaps spewing into the air, water churning. Dizzy, she felt so lightheaded.

The bastard had kissed her, before pushing her over the edge.

That was the last she remembered until she woke in the care of the Machiguengas.

"You don't need to understand." He swept his gaze over her and then the room still lit by candlelight. His ominous smirk made her gut twist, but it was the small switchblade he revealed that made her heart skip a beat. "I might not need this after all. No reason for rash action. We can just play out what it appears you already have planned."

"The hell we will." She lunged, body-slamming him.

Her goal—the knife.

It felt like she ran into a brick wall. He stumbled but didn't fall. As her arms came down on his, the knife flew out of his hand. Light bounced off the metal skittering across the floor, before it disappeared beneath the heavy dresser.

Allie didn't waste any time. Fingers curled into claws, she went for Tom's eyes.

He caught her wrists, releasing one to strike her sharply across the mouth. Pain burst in her jaw. Her palm rose to cover the throbbing area. She tasted blood, felt the wet warmth that touched her fingertips as it oozed between her lips.

Allie wasn't one to go down without a fight. She struck again. Catching him off guard, she swung a right to his midsection. Doubling over, he appeared stunned, giving her time to race for the door.

Tom was quick. Fisting his hand in her hair, he jerked. She flew backward with a cry. A burning sensation spread across her skull. It felt as if he had pulled every hair from her head, the bullet wound throbbing.

He yanked her hard against his chest, held her so tightly she couldn't breathe. His rapid breathing was hot against her neck. "I underestimated you. I won't do it again." He licked a path up her throat, making her want to vomit. "I see you found someone to indulge your lewd fantasies."

Gone was the man she had remembered. Instead, a madman held her in his grip.

"Well, Alison, your curiosity just might be the death of you." His voice dropped to menacing growl. "Nothing else has worked, not a cliff, gas, a bullet, or a car."

Gas? Tom had punctured the gas line—tried to blow her up?

Allie lost it.

Kicking and screaming, she struggled for freedom. Adrenaline surged through her veins, but it wasn't enough. He was bigger, stronger, dragging her toward the chains hanging from the wall. With a shove, he threw her to the floor. A heavy foot against her chest stole her breath.

His weight was paralyzing. She couldn't move.

Quickly, he unfastened the handcuffs from the chains. The second his foot rose, released her, she tried to suck in air. But found herself rolled faced down on the floor. The furry red manacles around her wrists, locked together.

The terrors of the jungle slammed into her, threatening to pull her back into their darkness. "No," Allie cried out, fighting its allure. If she was to survive, live, she had to keep her wits about her.

Focus. The jungle isn't real, but this is.

Her control disintegrated as Tom pivoted, holding the noose from Jake's treasure box in his hand.

Her mind screamed, "Jake."

ꕤꕤꕤ

"Where the hell are you?" Jake muttered, chugging down his third beer. He had waited long enough. Thomas King would just have to reschedule. Jake dug in his pocket and pulled out a twenty, throwing it on the table as he rose. He grabbed his cell phone, slipping it into his jeans as he made his way to the door.

Someone had turned the music up. Between it and the noisy crowd he was looking forward to a nice, quiet evening with the woman he loved.

The wind was blowing, the rain almost at a horizontal slant. Even if he had an umbrella, it would have been useless in this type of weather. Before he left the shelter of the restaurant, Jake pulled the edges of his jacket together, ducked his head and darted for his truck.

Standing in the pouring rain, he checked one pocket and then the other before finding his keys. His hands were shaking as he unlocked his truck and climbed in sopping wet. Retrieving his cell phone, he punched in his home number.

The first ring didn't bother him, it was the subsequent unanswered ones that chilled him to the bone.

Something was wrong.

Jake felt a sharp pain in his chest. Without delay, the engine roared to life. Cramming the truck into reverse, his pulse hastened. It grew faster as he tore out of the parking space. He floored it and he sped away.

A fountain of water exploded, submerging his truck as he hit standing water in his race to get home. A red light blared its warning. Glancing both ways, he darted through the traffic light. All the while, he prayed that Allie was all right.

The truck jumped the curb, bouncing him off the seat as he pulled into the driveway. He ignored the garage, parking outside and killing the engine. Like the wind, he was out of his truck and at the front door. He tried the knob. Locked. His hands shook as he used his keys and let himself in.

The house was quiet, except for the television. The fire had gone out in the hearth. There was a chill to the room. Towels lay upon the floor beneath a strange man's overcoat, which hung from Jake's coat rack.

Jake got a sick feeling in the pit of his stomach. Acid churned even more when he saw his robe laying on the stairs—a robe that Allie usually wore nothing else beneath.

There weren't any signs of struggle. No. From what he could tell, she had climbed those stairs of her own free will with another man.

Something inside his chest died. Anger took its place. Mounting the stairs two at a time, he first tried her room. It was empty. Slowly he turned toward his bedroom. The door was wedged open. He could smell the sweet scent of candles burning and see their flames flickering in the darkened room.

"Woman, you have some nerve." What a fool he was. His fingers clenched into fists. His legs were leaden as he headed toward what he was sure would break his heart in two—

Allie with another man.

Jake flung the door open, felt the air freeze in his lungs.

In the corner of his bedroom where the chains hung from the ceiling, Allie stood on a footstool wearing the black leather corset, thong, stilettos, fishnet stockings and fingerless gloves he had purchased for her several days ago. A ball gag was crammed into her mouth, her wrists handcuffed behind her, and a noose hung around her neck.

Even in the dim lighting, he could see that this wasn't a sensual scene. Allie eyes were rimmed red with fear. Her makeup smeared down her cheeks. She struggled to speak, but only made small, choking sounds. Pleading eyes and a jerk of her head, she tried to warn him, but it was too late.

Jake felt a stunning blow to the back of his head. Pain, darkness, and then splinters of bright light burst inside his head.

The force knocked him off balance. He stumbled, fighting to retain his footing. He heard Allie's muffled cries. Before he could fully recover, a man launched himself at him. The stranger struck with an intensity that tore both of them off their feet to land hard upon the floor.

"You sonofabitch. You're not supposed to be here," the man growled, increasing the pressure of his fingers around Jake's neck.

As they wrestled on the floor, Jake recognized the man as Thomas King, the client he was scheduled to meet tonight.

With a hard jab, Jake hit King in the ribs. A painful grunt and the man loosened his grip. Jake swung again, missing King as he rolled out of reach.

Dragging himself to his feet, Jake rushed toward Allie. If her foot slipped off the footstool she'd hang. Before he could reach her, King struck from behind, driving him to the side. He crashed into the dresser, whirling around to intercept a right to his jaw. There was a grinding of bone and tendons, and then he tasted blood. Jake ignored the pain, answering with a left that threw King stumbling backward.

From the corner of Jake's eye, he saw Allie's foot slide. The footstool tilted as she fought to gain purchase. Once again, he headed toward her, but a kidney punch dropped him to his knees.

Throbbing pain pierced the small of his back as he fought to breathe. Before he could inhale, King body-slammed him. Jake fell to the floor on his back, King falling atop him, hands closing around his neck.

Jake's lungs burned.

His vision dimmed.

He knew both his and Allie's lives depended on breaking the man's hold. Trying to free himself, Jake twisted and turned, then shoved his hands between King's arms, forcing them outward to break the hold.

Oxygen rushed Jake's lungs.

He curled into a ball. A powerful thrust, his legs connected with the sonofabitch's stomach, sending him flying through the air, arms flapping to protect his fall.

King hit the edge of the bed with a thud and a sickening crack.

Breathing labored, Jake crawled to his feet. King used the bed to steady himself and gain his footing.

Fists balled, Jake was ready for the man's next attack. What he wasn't ready for was King to dart away. Instead, he kicked the stool from beneath Allie's feet.

Terror raced up Jake's throat as the stool screeched across the floor. Allie dangled from the ceiling. Her feet jerked once, twice. A watery gurgle bubbled up from her throat.

She looked at him. Reddened eyes bulged. Tears seeped from their corners, before her eyes fluttered closed.

Jake hit a full run. He wrapped his arms around her thighs raising her so that the pressure against her throat was relieved. Her skin was cold, damp from perspiration.

He heard her gasp around the gag in her mouth.

Suddenly something hard struck his head. Sharp pain and darkness filled his mind, once again. He fought to keep a hold of Allie, fought to remain conscious, as he grabbed one of the chains hanging from the ceiling. If he was going down, the whole friggin' house was coming down with him.

Jake staggered, falling to the side. Several loud pops, the D-rings affixed to the ceiling and wall gave one right after the other. Balance off, he fell. Allie followed him down to the floor.

"Fuck," King screamed, as he threw the stepstool across the room. It crashed against the wall, breaking into pieces. "She just won't die."

Allie whimpered, straining against her bindings.

Disoriented, Jake moved slowly, his process awkward. He jerked the gag from her mouth. Her lips parted and she sucked down air like a fish out of water, before her eyes widened.

She screamed.

With a jagged leg from the stepstool in his hand, Tom lunged at Jake. Allie awkwardly rolled from atop Jake, crying out as the broken end of the stake sliced her arm. Fire spread up her limb, blood flowing freely.

None too gentle, Jake pushed her aside, grabbing Tom by his shirt and pulling him down. Allie landed on her shoulder, the dull pain nothing like the agony in her arm.

Her heart beat wildly. Wrists still handcuffed behind her, she could do nothing but watch.

Tom and Jake were locked into each other's arms, wrestling on the floor. Grunting and growling, they swung their fists. Some caught air; others made the most gruesome, grinding sound.

It was almost surreal in the dimly lit room with candles providing the only light.

Allie's throat felt raw and tender. Her arms and shoulders ached from being pinned behind her. The wound in her arm burned. But she had to do something. She gathered all the energy left inside her and jerked against her restraints.

Jake held Tom in a chokehold, striking blindly. Tom's hands fluttered, anxiously trying to gain release. An undercut to Jake's ribs made him loosen his hold. He grabbed for Tom, but the man was already running for the bedroom door.

He was trying to escape.

In a flash, Tom disappeared into the hall, Jake hot on his trail.

Allie was on her knees when she heard a curse and then a thud. Unsteadily, she got to her feet. As she entered the hallway, the two men broke apart.

What possessed Allie, she had no idea. Without thinking she smashed headfirst into Tom, driving him back against the banister.

Crack.

A piece of the railing gave way. Tom's eyes gaped. He lost his balance and tumbled off the staircase. Her forward momentum was so great that she followed him over the edge.

She was falling.

That sinking sensation swallowing her up halted with a sharp jerk.

It happened so fast.

Jake flung himself forward, hitting the floor. Desperately grasping, he nearly missed Allie's ankle.

King continued to fall.

There was a thud, a sickening crack, and then silence.

Allie wasn't a heavy woman, but fear and the fact that her wrists were still handcuffed, her free leg swinging, threw her weight off balance. As the tendons and muscles in his arms pulled tight, Jake prayed he could hold on.

Jake strained, grunting. Bracing his shoulder against the banister, he pulled Allie to safety and into his arms. She was cold to the touch. Her body trembled uncontrollably.

Quietly, he removed her handcuffs. She threw her arms around him, clinging to him as if she would never let go.

"Tom." Her voice was coarse and low. "Is he dead?"

Jake flinched with surprise. "You know him?"

"Ex-boyfriend."

Jake moved so he could glance over the broken railing to the man below. "Let's fucking hope the bastard's dead."

Tom didn't move. Blood pooled around his head. His leg lay in an unnatural position, twisted so his knee lay grotesquely in the opposite direction than it should have.

Jake's arm securely around Allie's shoulders, they headed for the stairs. As they reached the bottom step, Allie drew to a stop.

Jake released her and approached Tom, using the toe of his boot to nudge him in the side. He didn't move. Cautiously, Jake crouched, body tensed, ready to react if the bastard even stirred. He felt for a pulse.

"He's dead," Jake announced.

There were no tears in Allie's eyes, only an expression he couldn't read. Was she happy? Sad? Maybe it was relief.

Slowly, Jake rose. The only thing left was to call the police.

Chapter Twenty

It was finally over.

Allie sat next to Jake on the couch in his living room, their jeans-clad thighs touching. His arm draped protectively over her shoulders, while his fingers played aimlessly with the soft material of her green sweater. He had yet to stop glaring at Todd Granger, her ex-boss, who sat in her mother's recliner.

It had been three days since that horrible night. The police had found another car Tom had stolen a block away. Even as careful as he'd been, wearing gloves to avoid fingerprints and parking away from the house, his room key from the Red Roof Inn was discovered on the car's floorboard. Incriminating documents had been discovered, but the police would not elaborate on their contents.

Jake had insisted that he and Allie stay at the Hilton until after the police conducted their investigation. Later, he had a crew come in to clean the house and fix the banister.

This was their first day back home.

Allie glanced out the window to see nightfall. A big round moon hung in the sky with stars sprinkled about. The storm had disappeared with the rest of the turmoil in her life.

She and Jake were alive. Safe.

Jake gave her a squeeze. She looked up at him and tried to give him a reassuring smile. It failed, so she snuggled closer into the warmth of his body.

“Apparently, Tom has been working to destroy Brayer Tech since the company fired his father eight years ago. Thomas Ackland Senior committed suicide shortly after his dismissal,” Todd explained. “The economy had been bad that year. The company only did what thousands of other companies were doing to tighten their belts.”

“Easy for you to say,” Allie huffed. People’s lives meant nothing to big business. The old mighty buck was what drove them.

Todd ignored her sarcasm. “The recent explosion in Bulgaria, killing a scientist, was one of Tom’s jobs as well.” He straightened his backbone arrogantly. “It was only a matter of time before we discovered he was guilty.”

“In the meantime, neither Brayer Tech nor you thought twice about pinning it on me.” Allie couldn’t help the bitterness in her voice. In the last couple of days, her emotions had swayed from anger to hate for Brayer Tech and Tom, but there was also sadness.

Tom had been a victim too. He had lost a loved one from circumstances out of his control. His hatred had poisoned him.

“Now that all of this is over, Brayer Tech wants to offer you your old position in Peru.” Todd beamed proudly. “The company has kept the reassignment of this project quiet, but they think they might be able to salvage some of the research. So, what do you say—you in?”

Allie felt Jake tense beside her. He shifted nervously, yet he remained silent.

Todd’s grin deepened. “I’ve been authorized to offer you a fifteen percent raise.”

Bully. Bully. Throw the woman a friggin' bone and she was supposed to forget all that had happened?

Okay, she had to admit the chance to travel again was tempting. The fifteen percent raise was attractive. Yet Allie had found something much more appealing right here in her hometown—a man who loved her.

"Pass," she said.

Jake jerked his head around to stare at her. The expression of surprise that pulled at his face was priceless.

"You drive a hard bargain." Todd slapped his palms on his thighs. "Twenty percent, but I can't go any higher than that."

She gazed into Jake's golden eyes and saw her future. "Nope. I've got something better here."

Jake pulled her into a big bear hug, capturing her lips. Evidently, it didn't matter that another person was in the room. His mouth moved hungrily over hers before he released her.

"Come on, Allie, join us. You were the most efficient, thorough documentarian we have ever had," Todd insisted.

Did he speak the truth? Or was he packing sand up her ass because Brayer Tech had wrongfully accused her? Hell, there might even be a chance they owed her pay for the time she was lost in jungle.

"She said no." The rumble deep in Jake's throat warned that the discussion had ended.

Silently, Todd rose along with Allie and Jake. Todd held out his hand to Allie and she accepted it.

"Guess this is good-bye. If you ever—"

Jake's scowl was quick to quiet Todd.

He nodded in understanding, released Allie's hand, and without another word headed for the door.

When the door closed behind Todd, Jake harrumphed, "Finally." He dragged Allie into his embrace. "I didn't think that guy was ever going to leave." His expression softened, eyes bright with what looked like hope. "So, you've got something better here?"

Allie's stomach knotted. Jake had made his feelings known. The million dollar question remained. Was he looking for a lifetime commitment?

She took a shaky breath of courage. "If you'll have me."

"Have you?" He laughed as if she was being irrational. Suddenly, he grew silent. His voice was husky when he finally spoke. "Marry me?"

"What?" Had she heard him correctly?

"Marry me?" he repeated firmly. "Marry me and spend the rest of your life beside me. I want to wake each morning in your arms. Go to bed each night deep inside you. Say you'll marry me."

Could this really be happening?

Allie swallowed hard. Felt tears of joy touch her eyes. "Yes," she choked, fighting back emotion.

Jake jerked her off her feet, swinging her around, as he gave a heartfelt "Yahoo!" He set her on her feet, cupped her face between his palms, and he gazed deep into her eyes. "I've loved you forever, Alison Grant."

She pressed her mouth against his. Her lips slid across his, as she whispered, "I love you too."

"Show me?" His warm hands slipped beneath her sweater. He caressed her skin, moving his palms upward, dragging her sweater along. He kissed her softly, before jerking the sweater over her head. Cool air stroked her skin, goose bumps rising.

A glide of his hand, he grasped her ass and squeezed, before he leaned down and took one of her satin-covered breasts into his mouth. He teased her taut nipple with a bite and tug, leaving a wet spot where his mouth had been. With deft fingers, he twisted the back of her bra and it popped loose. He discarded it quickly, and then he captured the same nipple into his warm mouth.

"Jake." Allie arched into his touch. She reached down, taking her own breasts into her hands, lifting them higher in offering.

He glanced up and flashed a sexy grin that sent a shiver up her back, before he took her other nipple into his hot mouth. Over and over, he suckled, pulling and tugging, then finishing with a nip that made her gasp and tingles to shoot through her engorged breasts.

When he straightened to his full height, she plucked at the buttons of his shirt. One by one, she undid them, until firm muscle lay beneath her palms. He shrugged his shoulders, as she skimmed her hands along his chest. The shirt fell to the floor alongside her sweater and bra.

They came together, skin to skin—mouth to mouth.

His kiss was hungry and demanding, tongue nudging her lips before delving deep. All the while, he caressed up and down her arms, stoking the flame that burned inside her. She gripped his biceps, holding on and savoring his masculine flavor.

His finger dipped beyond her waistband to wedge down the cheeks of her ass. Warm, wet desire released between her thighs. The sweet, moist throb introduced a tightening low in her belly. Slowly, his finger rose, tracing a path along her waist, until he was directly beneath her bellybutton. Then he shoved his hand inside her jeans, pushing past her panties, and sinking a finger deep inside her.

Allie cried out at the sudden fullness. She pushed her feet apart, fumbling with the button of her jeans.

She needed more—much more.

As he finger-fucked her, moving in and out of her pussy, she shimmied out of her panties and jeans. Her tennis shoes stopped her clothing at her ankles. Frantically, she used one foot and then the other to remove her shoes, tearing off her socks, until finally she stood before Jake naked, ready and willing.

He released her and took a step backward. "Beautiful." Without words, he took her hand and led her around to the back of the couch. "Put your hands on the couch. I want to take you from behind."

Her heart was pounding. She loved this man. Whatever he wanted was his. She leaned over, placing her palms on the couch, exposing herself to him.

She heard his sharp intake, swearing she could almost feel the heat of his stare.

There was a thrill in not being able to see what was coming next. She started when his warm, wet tongue skimmed along her slit.

Ohhh...it felt so good.

Her body answered, releasing her juices as he lavished her pussy with one lick after another.

"You smell so delicious," he whispered before flicking his tongue against her clit, making the swelling bud beg for release. The muscles in her stomach tightened. A penetrating throb threatened to steal her breath. Her hips pushed against him, wanting him to carry her over the edge.

"Make love to me, Jake. I need you inside me." Instead of giving her what she begged for, Jake moved away. She glanced over her shoulder to see him staring at her. His face was flushed, his eyes dark with desire.

He raised his gaze to meet hers. "God, I love you." His voice was like sandpaper, rough and throaty. He ran a finger down her spine, sending goose bumps to cover her. "So beautiful." She felt him tremble beneath each cherishing stroke.

The way he shook with such passion squeezed her heart. "Now, Jake, take me now."

Jake's thought processes ground to a halt. He tried to inhale, but the pulsating between his thighs won. Pushing his jeans to his knees, Jake dug his fingers into Allie's hips. With one thrust, he entered her. Wet. Slick. Heavenly.

She was everything he'd wanted and more.

The short, breathy pants she freed matched his as he buried his cock deeper. He moved slowly at first, noting how her cradle held him tight. Her inner muscles squeezed him gently, encouraging him to ride her faster, harder. A shudder rippled through him and his hips set up a rhythm that matched the glide of hers.

When she released another groan, his ego took a giant leap. He couldn't believe how responsive she was.

And she was all his.

"Mine," he exhaled. "Say you're mine." By her own admission, he had to hear she surrendered to him body and soul.

Eyelids heavy with desire, she glanced over her shoulder. Her cheeks were flushed.

She was so sexy.

Blood filled his balls, drawing them tight against his body as he reached the melting point. He locked his jaw, fighting the climax ready to rip him asunder.

"I'm yours." Allie wet her lips, drawing his attention to her mouth. "Forever."

Her last word undid him. It was what he had dreamed of—wanted his entire life—Allie by his side, forever.

Violent and raw, his orgasm erupted. Liquid heat burned down his cock, shards of white-hot lightning. He couldn't have stopped it if he had wanted to. He thrust one last time, held her hips tight against his, and tumbled into ecstasy.

In the daze his mind had become, he heard Allie cry out. He felt the shudder that shook her as her body convulsed around his. Her soft whimpers wrapped around his heart and squeezed.

He needed to hold her—tell her how much she meant to him.

After she released a sated sigh, he eased away, pulled up his jeans, but left them unzipped. She rose from the couch, turned, and stepped into his embrace.

He gazed down at her. "I love you."

She snuggled closer, burying her head against his chest. "I love you."

The moment was perfect—all he could ask for. "I promise to make you happy."

She glanced up at him. "You already have." Her eyes glistened with unshed tears. "I'm finally home."

About the Author

A taste of the erotic, a measure of daring and a hint of laughter describe Mackenzie McKade's novels. She sizzles the pages with scorching sex, fantasy and deep emotion that will touch you and keep you immersed until the end. Whether her stories are contemporaries, futuristics or fantasies, this Arizona native thrives on giving you the ultimate erotic adventure.

When not traveling through her vivid imagination, she's spending time with three beautiful daughters, two devilishly handsome grandsons, and the man of her dreams. She loves to write, enjoys reading, and can't wait 'til summer. Boating and jet skiing are top on her list of activities. Add to that laughter and if mischief is in order—Mackenzie's your gal!

To learn more about Mackenzie, please visit www.mackenziemckade.com. Send an email to Mackenzie at mackenzie@mackenziemckade.com or sign onto her Yahoo! group to join in the fun with other readers and authors as well as Mackenzie!

http://groups.yahoo.com/group/wicked_writers/

Look for these titles by
Mackenzie McKade

Now Available:

Fallon's Revenge
Six Feet Under
Take Me
Bound for the Holidays
Lisa's Gift
Beginnings: A Warrior's Witch

Coming Soon:

The Perfect Gift: Second Chance Christmas
Black Widow

Driven to Distraction

© 2007 Ashleigh Raine

Dodging explosions, crashing cars, jumping off rooftops...and falling in love.

Up-and-coming stuntwoman Blaina Triton stops to help a sexy stranded stranger on the side of the road. Passion ignites hotter than the asphalt beneath their feet and they go back to his place for an anonymous carnal romp. Days later, she arrives on the set of her next feature film only to discover that the man she played out wanton erotic fantasies with is also her boss, Jay Williams. She thinks this job just got a whole lot better, until Jay makes it clear he never mixes business with pleasure.

Jay knows firsthand how distraction can be fatal, but around Blaina, his full, lust-ridden attention strays to her rather than staying on the job. In an effort to regain control, he offers an ultimatum—off set, their relationship is no-naughty-holds-barred, but on set, when they touch, it has to be strictly professional.

Soon their clandestine rendezvous ignite as hot as the movie's onscreen explosions. As an unstoppable stunt team, they are flawless, until the strain of their secret relationship begins to tear them apart. Jay has to make a decision. Walk away from the woman he loves, or allow himself to be driven to distraction...

Warning, this title contains the following: Jay and Blaina are imaginative in their proclivities. There's lots of sex in, on and around cars. Sex in public places, sex in a hotel room, masturbation, exhibitionism, oral sex, anal sex, spanking, minor bondage of the tie-me-up-and-have-your-wicked-way-with-me kind and sex with a foreign object.

Enjoy the following excerpt Driven to Distraction...

Without warning, Jay threw his car around a corner onto one of the small canyon roads. Like he could shake her that easily.

Whipping after him, she caught up as he pulled off in a turnout. Brake lights flashed as he came to a halt. She parked behind him, not even caring that the race had ended with him in the lead.

He stepped out of his car and she did the same, grinning from ear to ear. "Calling it a night already? You know I could've taken you—"

She froze in mid-sentence as he stormed toward her, eyes dark, body tight. All those hard sculpted muscles wrapped up in such a beautiful package, determinedly striding her way, like a predator ready to strike. Her natural fight or flight instinct kicked in, fiercely pumping adrenaline through her bloodstream, making her already hot body burn. But even as his chosen prey, there was no way in hell she was running away from him.

Jay drew to a halt a foot away from her, his chest rising and falling in rapid succession, his arms at his sides, hands curled into fists. Not angry. At least she didn't think so. Just tense. Powerful. His normal stance when he didn't have a clipboard, a tool or her breast in his hand.

Nipples growing tight, she crossed her arms over the announcement of her arousal and stared at his chest, remembering the way he looked standing naked in front of her. Sun-stained bronze liberally sprinkled with crisp golden curls, muscles tight beneath her exploring fingers. The Celtic flame tattoo that burned along his breastbone, adding an air of danger and intrigue that drew her in like a moth to a flame. Her fingers itched to rip off his blue T-shirt, to force him to show some emotion other than the steely gaze currently pinning her in place.

Blaina tilted her head back and met him stare for stare. "Are we just gonna stand here all night staring at each other?"

"Maybe."

His simple reply, or perhaps it was how he said it, a deep sizzling vibration of sound, had an annoying effect on her libido, making her stomach clench and toes curl. How sick was she that an indecisive word could make her pant like a dog in heat? If he said a full sentence would she hump his leg? Good lord, she was pathetic.

She blew out a furious breath, angry with both herself and Jay. Even knowing the consequences, she was ready to throw her brain and clothing out the window for one more chance to fuck him.

To avoid pulling him down to her level for a game of tonsil hockey, she tucked her hands in her back pockets. But her forced air of nonchalance had another side effect, thrusting her breasts, erect nipples and all, out in a "please fondle me" manner.

Jay inhaled sharply.

So the man could emote on occasion given the right stimulus. She tested her theory, leaning back against her car, keeping her breasts aimed outward and upward. His gaze followed her tits like they were bouncing black balls on karaoke night. It made her want to break out into song. Maybe "Damn, I Wish I Was Your Lover" would do the trick.

But making Jay deaf with her wailings wasn't exactly what she wanted to accomplish tonight.

He moved in close until the only way she could escape would be to climb over her car. As if she'd chance denting it like that. His gaze remained locked on hers. Blue had never been such a warm color before.

"You know, Jay, today was long and hot and tiring and as stimulating as this game of 'let's see who blinks first' is, I'm gonna have to—"

Before she could finish, his body met hers, sandwiching her between hard metal and even harder Jay. His calloused palms scratched over her bare arms, making her gasp, making her flesh ache for more, for deeper penetration, for her body to be consumed by his hands and mouth. She was ready to beg for him to end the torment, when his grip moved to her neck, tipping her head back.

"You blinked," was all he said before his lips ground down against hers, sucking away all rational thought. He devoured, tongue driving into her mouth with volatile force. In return, she dished out everything she had. Pouring into him, marking him, trying to ensure that come morning, he couldn't wipe her from his mind. She breathed his taste deep into her lungs, the raw male power that seeped from every pore.

But it wasn't enough. Clawing the wash-worn cotton of his shirt, her fingers dug into his pectorals and scraped down over a chiseled abdomen. Lower still, she grasped his bulging erection, feeling soft, faded denim and hard, relentless male.

His cock throbbed against her touch and she tightened her grip, circling his length through the forgiving fabric, fucking him with her hand. She purred and he growled, ripping his mouth from hers. "No. I won. It's my turn to take."

In fast, jerky movements, he undid her jeans, yanking them and her underwear down to her knees. He spun her around, pinning her against where her fender met her door, leaning toward the cowl, one hand against her spine holding her in place. With his other hand he traced down the crack of her ass and into the moisture seeping between her legs.

He paused there, swirling two fingers over her wet flesh, not quite entering. She wondered what he was waiting for. Her light was green and if he didn't race through her intersection at top speed, she'd implode.

She tried to spread her legs wider, anything to give him a clue that she wanted to be taken, but the hand pinned to her back and the jeans and underwear bunched at her knees kept movement to a minimum.

Those damn swirling fingers finally thrust their way inside and she just about hit peak velocity. He fucked her with his fingers like he would with his cock, slamming into her harder and faster, his leg pushing against hers, his hand flattened against and kneading her spine. She reached behind her, trying to grab him, to bring his body even closer. But his questing fingers slightly curled, adding an abrasive torment to the pleasure, and she completely surrendered, letting him control her like only he could, building her higher, making her not give a damn about being half naked against a car less than a block from the highway.

Stars burst in her vision when his thumb pressed against her anus. Oh God, she was going to die. She pushed back against his fingers on a strangled moan, wanting to scream but not wanting anyone to call the cops. It would be just her luck to get arrested for indecent exposure before she climaxed.

He removed his hand from her aching pussy. Denim rustled, a zipper lowered and plastic ripped. "So you like a man sliding in from behind, do you?" He traced his shaft up and down her aching slit, soaking his head in her juices, spreading the moisture between both cheeks. “Pinned to your rear, watching your ass move…”

She bit her lip, swallowed a moan and pretended to be one hundred percent in control. “That’s where he belongs.”

Printed in the United States
125571LV00004BA/283/P